"Confound it, I̶̶̶ ry order that I give d have done with y

"Go right ahead," Megan shouted. "Are you going to ask to bathe my wounds afterward?"

"What are you insinuating?" Justin demanded. "I have no need to importune innocent females. I am not a ravisher of virgins!"

"For that I am forever thankful, my Lord. Otherwise, this employment would be far too loathesome to me!"

Justin shook his head in incredulous fury. No woman had ever said that to him before. "Meggy, I could strangle you."

"Just don't ravish me," she retorted. Her anger faded into embarassment as she realized it was she who had expressed the first base thoughts . . . and she who almost wished he was in fact bent on seduction. . . .

Lady Megan's Masquerade

Cindy Holbrook

ZEBRA BOOKS
KENSINGTON PUBLISHING CORP.

ZEBRA BOOKS are published by

Kensington Publishing Corp.
475 Park Avenue South
New York, NY 10016

Second Printing: November, 1993

Printed in the United States of America

Chapter One

Rose Room Encounter

The Earl of Argyle strode along an upper passageway of his estate home, only to stop short when he heard a ferocious bellow emanating from the rose bedroom.

Frowning, he regarded the closed door with interest. The sound had resembled a wounded bull. Deeming it unlikely that he was hosting an expiring animal, he decided to investigate.

He swung wide the door to stand transfixed by what he saw. A rotund, round-faced little man pirouetted about in severe anguish, grasping his shin while miraculously howling and whimpering simultaneously. A white periwinkle wig swayed precariously on his head while various watch fobs danced in counter-rhythm to his bouncing belly.

"Ah . . . yes! Uncle Josepheth!" The Earl pronounced, enlightened. He had identified the bull. Then an inelegant sound that defied interpretation turned his eyes to the other occupant of the room.

Amidst a pool of ashes in front of a large, gracious

Adams fireplace, a shapely housemaid stood like an angry Titania rising from murky depths. She flourished a poker wickedly and her blue eyes flashed self-righteous fury. The effect of her Amazonian hostility, however, was diluted by the soot smudging her fair complexion and dusting her hair, honey under a madly askew mobcap. A drab maid's dress enveloped her, except where the torn neckline careened off one rounded, creamy-white shoulder.

"The bull and a kitten?" the Earl murmured. Then, more loudly, he inquired in a deep, lazy voice that always tended toward amused boredom, "What, pray tell, is going on in here?"

The little man halted in mid-howl and swung out of his dance to hobble indignantly over to the Earl.

"Justin, my boy! Sack the wench. The blasted chit actually took a poker to me! Demme near broke my leg off, she did!"

"Now why, dear Uncle, would she choose to do a thing like that?" Justin drawled wickedly.

"I . . . harrumph . . . was merely offering her a courteous word," scowled Uncle Josepheth, avoiding his nephew's discerning eye.

"Oh?" The Earl's dark eyebrows lifted, "I'd hazard it was more like a slip on the shoulder."

The maid gasped in consternation and quickly pulled her garment up over her shoulder, unaware that this promptly exposed her indecorously, but flatteringly, at the front.

"But that ain't no cause to slice at me with a bloody poker!" Uncle Josepheth blustered, offended. "The way she was swinging about was damned dangerous. The wench nearly unmanned me! Why, when I was young, a gel like that would have been flattered by my attendance."

"Yes, Uncle, I have no doubt of that," Justin smiled,

6

"when you were young."

"Harrumph . . . well I've still got a lot of spirit in me, by Gad," Josepheth retaliated stiffly.

The Earl could have sworn, he heard a sotto voce "Sasa," from the housemaid's direction. He glanced at her, only to see her standing quietly, head demurely bowed over her poker, which she held as if playing a polite game of croquet.

"And in my day," Uncle Josepheth continued, squinting at her suspiciously as he limped toward the door now held open for him by the Earl, "young men had proper respect for their elders. They would have been horsewhipped for such insolence as yours. And the chit the same! Insubordination! What is the world coming to? Young ones just pussyfooting around. No blood and flesh in the lot of them. Harrumph . . .".

Justin wryly closed the door on a tirade prophesying the world's dandified decline. Leaning his broad shoulders against the doorframe, he took a long, considering look at the maid, noting every detail from her blackened mobcap to her sooted boots.

Slow respect gleamed in his eyes. She did not fidget. She did not twitter. Certainly this kitten was not of the nervous persuasion.

"What is your name, lass?" the Earl asked.

". . . Meggy, sir," she answered in a thick country brogue that was strangely well-modulated and lyrical.

The Earl's expression sharpened at the absence of the scratchy rasp common to the local folk. He watched her sketch a creditable curtsy, still armed with the poker. The unattended neckline slid off her other shoulder.

"My apologies for my misdirected uncle," he drawled pleasantly, never removing his eyes from her. "I pray you will excuse his execrable manners. As he stated, in his salad days such an offer was considered flattering." The Earl paused. "Not that it is much different today. Perhaps he could not resist your beauty."

The girl neither fluttered, gurgled, giggled, nor cooed, all very proper and expected responses to his flattery. Instead she stood and returned a shrewd, considering gaze much like his own.

Meggy saw before her an awe-inspiring man—tall, broad-shouldered, and slim-hipped. Definitely a Corinthian, she mused. Yet the sartorial set of his cravat and his compelling savoir-faire surpassed that classification. Truly a nonpareil, she admitted to herself.

Grey lightly winged his raven-black hair with distinction. A fine aristocratic nose graced the angles and planes of his chiselled face. His lips were perfectly sculptured, a blatant sensuality in his otherwise cool and reserved features.

His eyes were water-grey, fringed with absurdly long, feminine lashes and marked with dark, flaring brows. The water-grey was pierced with shards of hazel that deepened with the intensity of his gaze. As the full force of that gaze penetrated her concentration, she started out of her musings.

"I sincerely hope he did not frighten you," the Earl murmured.

"Not much," Meggy returned a quick half-grin. "It was rather like an attempted ravishment by Father Christmas."

Justin couldn't fathom the wave of feelings suddenly washing through him. Perhaps it was the glint of such ocean-blue eyes, or possibly Uncle Josepheth's blood was just now surfacing in his veins, but a wildly mischievous urge was taking hold of the arrogant Earl of Argyle.

"Perhaps you would like to know how it is being ravished by a man, rather than a Christmas saint," he suggested with an unholy gleam in his eyes. He strode forward purposefully.

The poker flew into a fighting position and Meggy emitted one unladylike expletive. "The devil!"

"Only too true, m'dear," the Earl agreed, stalking toward her with stealthy, feline grace. Not a tame feline, either, but a jungle cat.

"Do leopards smile like that?" Meggy wondered to herself as she retreated nervously. Unfortunately, she, like even the best generals, found that a quick retreat had backed her into a corner, or rather, a fireplace.

The fireplace mantle refused to yield, but as she sidled alongside it, she met the irons. They clanked and clattered to the floor in loud surrender, and Meggy and her trusty poker followed.

Justin stopped, surveying the indignant figure on the floor, pokers, irons, and brooms crisscrossing every which-way around her. He lost control and doubled over in fits of laughter.

"Why, you cur!" Meggy sputtered in outrage. "You big lout! You . . . you . . .". She suddenly sputtered into choking and thence into fits of giggles as she realized the situation. "You clod!" She laughed.

"Here, let me assist you," Justin chuckled. He gingerly stepped into the clutter and reached down his hand to her.

"Why, certainly, my Lord," Meggy agreed with sweet malice. She kicked an iron at his feet to unbalance him and swiftly jerked him forward. He toppled next to her with a decisive thud.

"Ooff!" was Justin's first word as he hit the Aubusson carpet. He slowly rolled over and pinned her with a cold, stern look.

Meggy drew in a quick breath and propped herself up on her elbow to look at him better, her torn bodice resting even more precariously on her shoulder.

Suddenly, effervescent bubbles coursed through her and despite the danger, she exclaimed dramatically, "Oh no, it's bellows to mend for me!"

An arrested expression froze Justin's aristocratic features until he perceived, and groaned at the atrocious pun. Then he laughed as he shifted his weight off the pierced leather of the bellows lying beneath him. A cacophony of giggles and guffaws filled the room.

"I have decided not to give you the pleasure of being ravished—you are much too enervating, my dear." Justin's tone feigned the lazy dandy. "Besides, I do not have affairs with the lower orders."

"I know." Meggy nodded her head in deep satisfaction, like a cat with a canary well between its teeth. Justin, Earl of Argyle, was known for his fastidious taste in women. Many judged him terribly high-in-the-instep, but his intimates knew it was a point of honor. He preferred to confine his affairs to women of his own class, or the sophisticated highflyers who knew the rules of the game. To dally with the lower classes was to abuse his station.

"How do you know?" The Earl ill-liked her obvious pleasure.

"Well, because . . . well." Meggy hesitated, suddenly abashed. "Because I've heard the gossip. You only have the high-flyers of the first stare. Diamonds of the first water . . . They must be very expensive, I should wager." She was considering the matter with due care.

"You are an impertinent upstart," Justin said stiffly, "listening to backstairs gossip!"

"But of course, my Lord," Meggy replied reasonably.

Justin bounded up as Meggy brought home the inanity of what he had said. Was she truly innocent, or was she being insubordinate? He stopped suddenly at the door and turned to ask curiously, "By the way, were you truly seeking to break my uncle's leg with

10

that poker?"

"Oh, no!" Meggy exclaimed with studied innocence. "It was very poor aim, my Lord, very poor aim indeed."

Justin smiled slightly.

"May I say for my uncle, you unman the both of us, Meggy." He bowed in ironic grace and exited, leaving Meggy staring after him.

Meggy picked herself up and went to work with a will. If Uncle Josepheth didn't get her sacked, the state of the bedroom would. As she picked up the fallen weapons, she thought over recent events. Being a housemaid was certainly difficult, if one's virtue was forever being assailed. How did other serving maids manage it?

She would certainly chide Mr. Tothwell; she was surprised that his hawk-eyes had overlooked such a jolly reprobate as Uncle Josepheth. He was a character befitting a note in the annals of history. She smiled mischievously as she remembered his red-faced blustering when he clapped eyes upon the poker. He had gone cross-eyed watching it.

No, Uncle Josepeth hadn't worried her. He was a lovable lecher. Mr. Tothwell's mistake about the Earl disturbed her more. He had informed her that the Earl was highly respectable, and never dallied with the lower classes. If their recent encounter was an example of his respectable behavior, she would not care to be present if he decided to throw his reserves to the winds.

Yes, it appeared Mr. Tothwell had made some misjudgement; she could see his eye glass slipping right now. A gentle smile tipped Meggy's lips as her memory replayed her first meeting with the eminent member of Ramsey, Tothwell, and Wordsworth. She once again sat in his chair and heard the shock in his voice. . . .

"Oh, I say!" Mr. Tothwell's glass fell from his

protruding eye, blurring the offending document before him. As an agent of his illustrious firm, he prided himself on his unshakeable English composure and unflagging Tothwell preciseness. One could be sure there was never a thread loose on his serviceable grey suit or a hair astray on his slightly balding head.

Today, however, was the day to shake his composure. No national financial disaster was responsible. Nor was it noticeable that the world's demise was at hand and all its occupants called to account. No, it was an unofficious document of legal gender.

"My Lady, surely this cannot be! Why, he must have been dicked in the nob, his attic to let! I mean—age must have severely dimmed his wits. Ah no, I mean he could not have been in control of all his faculties—I mean—"

"I believe I know what you mean," Megan, Viscountess of Marchington, said, humor gently ruffling her voice.

Mr. Tothwell groped frantically for his glass, accidentally pulling a coat button and entangling his hand with his watch fob. His next convulsive grasp landed his quarry and he popped the errant glass back into his startled, myopic eye. His vision clearing, he focused on yet another vision.

The lady before him was tall, with a trim, pleasing figure. Dressed in a morning dress of willow green with double flounces at the hem, bordered by pale lavender velvet ribbons wound in Dresden lace, she looked a veritable dream.

Beneath the fetching straw bonnet secured jauntily by a deep purple silk bow, Megan Linton's deep blue eyes, clear complexion, and tawny blond hair enhanced features that were classically beautiful. In repose, she could have posed for a statue of a Greek goddess, but such a statue would never be—Lady

12

Linton also possessed a wide, mobile mouth that totally upset all that was classic. Within a twinkling, it could turn from cool humor into a remarkable crooked grin.

Her eyes, fringed with dark, honey-tipped lashes were not those of Athena tranquilly surveying humanity, but changing whirlpools of emotions and ideas. Yet she could appear every inch the lady. Her grandfather fondly called her his hoyden-in-hiding.

The Viscountess' voice was firm and cool. "My grandfather was an eccentric, Mr. Tothwell, but no one could say that he was not in his right mind."

"You are not going to contest this will?" Mr. Tothwell was not only surprised, but somewhat irritated at her composure. "I do not believe you comprehend the full terms, my Lady. In effect, to gain his fortune you must demean yourself and become a common serving maid!"

"Need it be a common one?" Lady Linton interrupted, eyes wide.

Mr. Tothwell, intent on painting for her the evils his orderly mind envisioned, plunged onward. "One of the lowest! You would have to live in drudgery for six months, and what is beyond all conception is that you would live on a servant's pay! Why, it is unseemly! Unthinkable! No lady would submit to such an outrage!"

"This lady will," Megan replied quietly.

Mr. Tothwell sucked in his breath, trying to gather the shattered pieces of his composure before blurting out, "The man must have been daft!"

"I *must*, and *will*, follow his desire. I will not contest the will." There was a quiet edge to her voice.

In the stunned silence that followed, Megan remembered the lost, hurt child who had clung to the old man when her parents died at sea. He, likewise, had clung to

13

her. She had possessed her mother's and father's love for five years.

Her parents had been adventurers and somehow, amidst the pain and fear, she had known that they had not meant to leave her. They had simply gone on an adventure and, through no fault of their own, were unable to return. She liked to believe that they were still adventuring, only it was a different kind, where no letters were written home.

That was when the leathery hand of Grandfather John had reached out to clasp her tiny, frightened one. The soul of the little girl Megan quickly understood the spirit of Grandfather John.

John Linton was a man out of step with his time. He had waltzed before the dance was even whispered in Almacks.' He studied Regency life and saw something different. He did not believe his birth gave him powerful rights over others; it was his education and opportunities, not his bloodline, that created him. That masses of people could be left in the dungeons of ignorance and the gloom of the workhouse appalled him; no sophistry could excuse it. All men had the same needs and the blood flowing in their veins, either blue or red, could not change that.

Despite such shocking beliefs, John Linton was neither a politician nor a revolutionary. He harbored no desire to go haring about the countryside instigating riots or insurrections, for he had complete faith that compassion would prove victorious in the end. When the Almighty grew weary of man's tiddlywinks and barriers, He would, with one exasperated sigh, blow those barriers down.

Until then, John Linton would strive to be the man he thought he should be. He would be kind to his servants. he would—to the horror of his peers—offer them education. He had left London society years before, when his beloved Kate had died, and this enabled him to work within his village to develop the utopia of which he dreamed. Needless to say, he was the shire's reigning eccentric.

The young bundle named Megan had come as a blessing and a joy. Set apart from his colleagues by his stubborn refusal to accept the "understood", John Linton had become a lonely man. He saw the open, curious child begging to be enlightened, and he obliged with as many colours as possible.

The role of society women severely disappointed him. How could an uneducated lady make a competent mother or companion? Furthermore, it seemed obvious to him that women starved of all mental occupation must inevitably become bored silly; the many pretty, prudish widgeons adorning society were positive, twittering proof. Husbands, forced to wake up to such sheltered vapidness—unless nodcocks themselves—would naturally cut out to those others who at least were allowed a street education. In the wife-mistress game, John Linton deemed, the wives never started out with a full deck of cards in the first place.

His Megan was not to suffer such a fate. She would have the right to study whatever she desired. To his deep delight, his little Megan truly desired and she jumped every educational hurdle he threw in her way.

She learned the accomplishments of a lady as well as the knowledge of the gentleman. Literature enthralled her. Politics amused her. Aiding the village doctor challenged her.

She was master of the pianoforte and the petit point; she could also ride the wildest horse and catch the slyest trout. She understood the science of boxing, possessing a decent left for her weight, but the art of the duel was her favorite, captivating her with its grace and

15

intricate movements.

Lady Megan and Lord John were two mischievous idealists romping in the playground of Linton Manor, separated from the world around. When Lord John died, Megan knew that she had lost a kindred spirit, a true knight. Perhaps the good Lord's paradise would offer him better material for his utopia.

However, he had left her behind to deal with his last brainchild—to live six months as a maid. Why had he done it? He had written that he desired her to understand the life of the lower orders so she could manage her vast fortune and properties better after this.

At first, Megan felt only pain. Did he not believe in her compassion for her fellow man? But as the pain subsided, her common sense reasserted itself. He had always believed in her—that could not be the reason.

Grandfather John had never been a revolutionary. Why did his will apparently force her to become one? Perhaps, she thought ruefully, she was to be his one and only attempt. If so, she hoped he was taking note from his ghostly sphere on this, his last and only revolutionary battle cry.

Though Megan did not realize it, her fighting instincts had forged to the front. This request, so un- usual and challenging, called forth all her resources. Not every young debutante sallied forth as a serving girl—the idea appealed to her. Nay, it thrilled her. What a lark! The frozen, lost woman became a lady with a purpose.

Megan finally returned her gaze to Mr. Tothwell, who was peering at her in concern. "Mr. Tothwell, there is no use in dithering over whether or not I can do it."

Mr. Tothwell stiffened. He never "dithered."

"It must be done. I must admit Grandfather has set

16

me an extraordinary task and I have no understanding of his reasoning, but reasoning I'm sure he had. I would never try to overset my grandfather's will, so there are many necessary arrangements. First, I must find a post at an establishment."

"Ah—yes, my Lady," Mr. Tothwell agreed resignedly. "Where should this post be? Have you considered the possiblity of recognition?"

"Yes, I have. Fortunately, I never made my official coming out in London. Grandfather did not believe in throwing young girls into the arena of society so early. He always considered it a modern form of virginal sacrifice."

"My Lady!"

"Yes, I know, it is rather a strong view," Lady Megan conceded with a twinkle. "But it means I have not gone about much. If we can find the right post at an out-of-the-way establishment, we may scrape by."

"I see what you mean, my Lady," Mr. Tothwell said, grudgingly intrigued.

"No one knows of the will except Mr. Ramsey, to whom it was sent, you, and myself. I have it on the best authority that you are very circumspect, with a natural eye for detail. I believe you can find me that perfect position. Grandfather did not stipulate the type of establishment; I do not see that it need be a poor one— or one where I must be in deathly fear of the master. In fact, if I could find an uninhabited, unvisited one, that would be ideal. I may still wish to go to London after this adventure and I hope to avoid being hailed as 'the Right Honorable So-And-So's maid.' I will need references, ideas on how to enter and exit my post, and a myriad of other details. I hope you can help me. Can you?"

Mr. Tothwell only stared. What an extraordinary lady! And if she wanted detail and precision, he admitted, she had come to the right man. The idea of a lady incognito as a maid was absurd, but he might just be able to arrange it. "There is so much to think on."

"Exactly so. Well, Mr. Tothwell?"

"Yes, my Lady, I will do it. It may take me some time—but consider it done!"

. . . "And so it was done," murmured Megan, as she left her memory to stare disconsolately at the huge ash spot she had just discovered on the fine brocade chair.

Cinderella had had her fairy godmother, Megan her Mr. Tothwell. Within a remarkably short time he had produced a wonderful opening for her at one Argyle Court. How he had found a position so quickly still astonished Megan. He had looked somewhat smug—though that might have been a trick of her imagination, so fleeting was the look—and explained that he had his own connections.

He had explained proudly that the court was certainly an out-of-the-way spot, as its lord and master rarely visited it; Justin Maximillian Marcus Stanton Devenish was a government diplomat. Furthermore, he was a gentleman. He never dallied with the help. His pride on that point was even recognized within his own circle.

Ha! Megan thought. Apparently his discretion served more than his country. This she would not tell Mr. Tothwell. She still kept in contact with him, something he had insisted on before he would help her. The horse trading between them on such details outdid any business performed at Tattersalls.'

Mr. Tothwell promised her references if she promised to stay in contact. He promised that no matter what occurred, he would not interfere (that would have transgressed the terms of the will in Megan's mind) as

18

long as she took her groom, Jed, along. Mr. Tothwell had, like some magician, pulled out references for him, too. This concession had been extremely hard for Megan to agree to, though she admitted now she was grateful for it. A story that Jed was her fiancé explained their constant communication and saved her from the downstairs Romeos.

Yes, Mr. Tothwell had created a perfect situation for her, as far as being a serving girl went, and he had been a martinet in drilling her on her fabricated life history, and her speech and manner. His eye for detail was magnificent, if not merciless.

Now she would see if their story held together; certainly it seemed it would be a trial by fire. First, to upset their most perfect plan, Lady Augusta, the Earl's mother, had arrived. Then Uncle Josepheth. Then the Earl of Argyle himself. Let the polite world think what it would, the Earl was no gentleman.

"Oh, Mr. Tothwell," Megan moaned, "truly, the best of plans do go awry." She bent and picked up the last fire iron and clutched it to her in sudden presentiment. What else could go awry? No, she shook her head, she didn't want to know.

Chapter Two

Tangled Threads

Wisely ignoring the question of her future, Megan set her mind on the more pressing problem of saving her position, as unenviable as it was. Perhaps if she talked to Mrs. Bodkins she could glean some advice upon that ticklish subject. She absolutely refused to lose her job and fortune over either an irascible libertine or an arrogant panther.

Sighing, she gathered up her tools and walked back to the kitchen where Mrs. Bodkins could usually be unearthed. Megan had come to admire and trust the spirited, buxom little Irish woman. Mrs. Bodkins was a special blend of competence and kindness.

Lady Luck, after her shrewish desertion all day, smiled upon Megan; she found Mrs. Bodkins in the kitchen, watching Cook's baking. Excellent, Cook must be in the pantry. Mrs. Bodkins was scratching out a list, accompanying her writing with an Irish ditty.

"There ye be, lass," Mrs. Bodkins chimed in greeting. "Did ye finish the rose—Faith! What happened to ye? Did ye fall in the fireplace, girl? Ye were to take the

20

ashes out of the grate, not join them."

"Mrs. Bodkins, please let me explain," Megan said. "It was either join the ashes or join a certain Uncle Josepheth . . . in the bed. I. . . ."

"Saints above, I forgot about him. He arrived this morning. I forgot to warn ye. Ah well, I see I needn't to, now. 'Tis plain ye've had the pleasure." Mrs. Bodkins stifled a smile at Megan's blackened appearance.

"I would not call it a pleasure, but yes, I have met him," Megan said severely.

"He did not harm ye, did he lass?" Mrs. Bodkins asked, her smile sliping into alarm.

"No, mum," Megan quickly assured. Striking a fateful pose and raising one limp wrist to her forehead, she declaimed, "Alas, I nearly fainted, so overset was I. I have such delicate nerves you see, such refined sensibilities. But just before I succumbed—to faint, that is—I defended myself with a poker! What was a poor maiden to do?"

"Oh, God love ye!" exclaimed Mrs. Bodkins "It's just what that old rasher of wind deserves. Ever since I was a young girl workin' here, he's been chasing the maids. His hands wander more than travelling minstrels, always makin' me lose me best help when he visits. Well, I hope ye used that poker something like!"

"How bloodthirsty, Mrs. Bodkins," Megan gasped in delight. "But no, that was not necessary. I did swipe at him once, but then the Earl arrived—another family member you didn't warn me about."

"Is me boy home?" Mrs. Bodkins jumped up in delight. "We didn't expect him till yonder. Ye never know when he's to arrive. Even when he says so, he doesn't. So he rescued ye, did he, lass? Isn't he a proper hero?" she sighed, starry-eyed.

"More like an improper one," Megan murmured. But Mrs. Bodkins was much too ecstatic to notice, so

21

Megan agreed dryly, "Yes, a true gallant."

"Now there's a lad ye never have to fret about. Just the opposite of that no-good uncle of his. Always respectful, always pleasant. He makes workin' for him a true delight."

"You don't say," Megan choked, bewildered. Everyone, even the insightful Mrs. Bodkins, declared the Earl to be the epitomy of respectability, as safe as a puppy. But she'd place him in the full-grown wolf category, rather than the domestic breed.

"Ah yes, a fine man, the Earl. Not saying that all the lassies aren't a-hopin' he'll look their way," Mrs. Bodkins observed, very much the contented hen proud of her chick. "I wonder what brought him here. I'm surprised he could tear himself away from that Malissa Rambington." Mrs. Bodkins almost snorted in disgust.

"Who's Malissa Rambington?" Megan asked, interested despite herself.

"A snooty, coldhearted Jezebel, that's who she is. They call her a lady, no less. A widow. Ha! She had the widow's weeds already sown and packed with her trousseau. The old earl was seventy-five when she sunk her talons into him. She has the heart of a common trollop," Mrs. Bodkins spouted, her Irish temper riled. She scratched and rescratched the list she was writing, so fiercely that Megan was sure the table bore the impressions.

"Ye should see the diamonds and horses and carriages she demands. Oooh, she's got a selfish streak the width and length of her back, but Master Justin only sees her beautiful face."

"I'm sure that's not all of her he sees," Megan commented dryly. "Though I'd think he'd have discovered that selfish streak by now, if it is on her back."

This sally arrested the Irish woman's fulminations.

She blinked and tutted. "Now, dearie, ye shouldna be talkin' like that. I shouldna' be blethering such things to a sweet lass like ye, but ye shouldna' be understanding what I mean. I know there's no harm in ye, but someone might take ye wrong. Now go clean up and come back to serve her Ladyship's tea. Right now, ye look a very chimney urchin."

Mrs. Bodkins watched Megan's graceful exit with a deep frown. What was to come of all this? The girl was pluck to the backbone, but such a confusing mixture of naiveté and knowledge. How could her grandfather have done this to her!

Yes, Mrs. Bodkins knew who her pert maid truly was. As second cousin to Mr. Tothwell on his father's side, it was only natural. She was Mr. Tothwell's "connection."

At first, when she had read his missive asking for her help, she could not believe such a fantastic situation. But Mr. Tothwell was not one subject to flights of fancy, and if he said the young lady was hell-bent on her course and he could not, in all conscience, deter her, then it was so.

Mrs. Bodkins certainly planned to follow Mr. Tothwell's instruction never to let Lady Megan know. That intrepid Lady's pride would not allow it. Mr. Tothwell had studied the terms of the will closely and in no way, he wrote, was he breaking them. Whether Lady Linton would have agreed would never be put to the test, for the secret would remain between the two relatives. Certainly the old adage held true: what Lady Linton didn't know couldn't hurt her. In fact, with the rocky course that lay before her, it could only help.

A half hour later and a few shades lighter, Megan edged open the parlor door with her foot, her hands overly occupied with a large silver tea tray. One shoulder twitched rebelliously against her all-encompassing dress which, though reined in with a little pinning and stitching, was nonetheless voluminous. Arrested, she stopped to gaze at the room, studying the honey-toned drapes pulled back by gold braiding. Sunlight beamed through the terrace windows, adding a warm glow to the Axminister carpet. She sighed, appreciating the refined choice of objets d'art so contrary to the attitude of the day of strewing bibelots in every direction. Two large oriental vases flanked the double entrance doors opposite the wall containing the fireplace with its Adams mantle.

On a settee of watered silk sat a petite older woman dressed in black. The delicate woman mellowed the somber colour—so often severe on older women—until it glowed. Fine lines traced themselves along her face, crinkling at her eyes and dancing up the sides of her mouth. A halo of silver hair wisped about her head.

Her eyes, which Megan hazarded were blue, peered sternly at her needlepoint while her delicate hands, nervous as startled doves, fluttered restlessly over it.

Megan tiptoed over and set the tray down on the table in front of the sofa. She dipped a curtsy and awaited dismissal. There was a complete silence.

Her Ladyship pursed her lips and pulled a scarlet thread through the linen. This was hard going, thought Megan.

"Is there anything else Her Ladyship desires?" Megan asked hesitantly. She shot another curtsy, starting to feel like a bobbing top.

Still there was nothing but the silence of a mausoleum. Megan thought of leaving, regardless of Mrs. Bodkins' instructions to never depart without dismissal. She certainly would not be dismissed, since she had never been recognized. Yet Megan proved to

24

be a conscientious, if not stubborn, maid. She tried again. This time though, after clearing her throat rather forcefully, she intoned in a stentorian voice, "Her Ladyship's tea."

As the teacups rattled on the tray from the vibrations, she bounced her curtsy, deeming it fine practice.

Success appeared. Her Ladyship gazed up with vague, bright blue eyes. Ha! Megan was right, her eyes were blue, though unfocused.

"Ah yes, put the tray down," Lady Augusta directed pleasantly.

Megan was stumped. She looked at the service tray, already resting upon the table, with something close to reproach. How could she follow Lady Augusta's one demand now? Perhaps she should pretend to do so, so as not to countermand the orders.

This niggling worry was chased away by the grim realization that her Ladyship was once again peering at her stitching. No dismissal floated from her puckered lips.

Oh no, did she have to repeat all those infernal curtsies? But no, a flustered murmur arose from her Ladyship.

"I am simply making a terrible mull out of this. Dear me, these threads tangle themselves up so promptly. It just does not look the thing. What do you think, my dear?" she demanded.

Unsure of what to think, Megan eased around the settee and studied the piece over Lady Augusta's shoulder. Megan was still unsure what to think.

A burst of bright reds and yellows assaulted the eyes in blinding glory. It seemed an explosion of no mean order. Megan rejected this theory, deeming it an unlikely subject for lady Augusta's drawing room

"Well, what does it look like?" fretted her Ladyship,

still tugging at the tangled thread.

"Is it a sunset?" queried Megan, nervously. She had had no idea that a housemaid's life encompassed so many dangers.

"Oh dear, I was hoping it was not as bad as all that," sighed Lady Augusta. "It's a peony. I've tried to follow the tracings, but these threads continue to knot, and I am never sure what color to use. Is the shading at fault?"

The shading could not truly be said to be at fault for the simple and remarkable reason that there was no shading, merely battling colors clustered in florid splotches. However, Megan, understanding the difficulties of needlepoint for those who did not possess the knack of it, swallowed and smiled bravely.

"Yes, ma'am, I do believe it is," she perjured and encouraged. "Perhaps if you use a different stitch, you can define the peony."

"A different stitch? Good, for I am very weary of this one. It is not comfortable at all. Do show me," Lady Augusta asked eagerly. Megan hesitated, unsure of a proper housemaid's duties. Lady Augusta had made such a muddle of the sunset-peony, however, that Megan felt obliged to assist her. Indeed, after another glance at that awesome creation, she felt compelled. Deciding to call her Ladyship's plea a command, she settled down next to her.

"Well, my Lady, first we will unknot this thread. Then perhaps we will use another color with the stitch I mentioned. . . .

As her Ladyship was eager to learn, both ladies were soon vigorously intent upon the peony's reformation.

This was how the Earl discovered them. He had planned to surprise Lady Augusta. She surprised him.

Finding her lost in needle point was no extraordinary thing, for she did battle with the frame constantly. Finding a housemaid cozily at work beside her did surprise him. It simply was not done in the best households. And not just any old maid, but Uncle Josepheth's maid at that.

Neither woman had heard him enter, so busy were they examining threads—her ladyship's a bright orange, Meggy's a deep rose hue.

Justin stopped and watched through lidded eyes. This maid was becoming a mystery.

When he had gone to ready himself for tea, he had happened to ask his valet, Tuttle, if he had heard anything about a new maid-in-residence. Tuttle had stopped and stared in bewilderment at the query. The Earl of Argyle never asked about the menial staff. Indeed, Tuttle had not heard of the new maid, offering a sniff to emphasize the fact that he did not deal with such low denizens.

All the more curious, Justin had sent Tuttle downstairs to find some answers. He still remembered Tuttle's frigid hauteur as he reported, "Mrs. Bodkins says she is a new upstairs maid, hired just recently. She also says that they have hired her fiancé . . . a groom, in the stables, my Lord. That is all she said, my Lord. He sniffed. "Will that be all, my Lord?"

Justin was even more intrigued. It was an odd report in that it was so very brief; usually Mrs. Bodkins was a garrulous informant who knew the ancestry of every servant back twenty-five generations, and said so.

Further pressed, Tuttle, that much-offended dignitary, had added, "Mrs. Bodkins said she was a good girl, my Lord. Will that be all, my Lord?"

Justin, still unsatisfied but aware of his valet's mottled color, dismissed Tuttle so that that worthy could succumb to the apoplexy he so patently desired.

The object of Justin's inquiry and Tuttle's upset was just saying to her noble protégé, "My Lady, what we need is some shadowing. This darker color should do the trick. Let us wait and use that . . . fine . . . brilliant yellow in a different place."

"And what are we doing now?" Justin asked in a pleasant voice. It seemed he had been asking that a lot lately.

He directed his gaze toward Megan, who looked up wide-eyed, a rose thread dangling from nerveless fingers. Frozen, she stared at the Earl, who gazed back enigmatically. Having botched his role as St. George earlier, he intended to show her that he was civil and proper now.

"Oh Justin, the maid is showing me how to make shadows. Isn't that kind of her?" Lady Augusta enthused. Turning to Megan, she pronounced proudly, "My dear, this is my son, Justin. Justin, this is ah. . . ." A look of bafflement crossed Lady Augusta's face.

"Meggy," the Earl supplied. Her Ladyship looked at Megan, who nodded in agreement.

Lady Augusta smiled happily. "Yes, certainly." Justin grinned. His mother was vague with such aplomb.

"Come, sit down and have some tea. I didn't know you were to arrive today. I thought it was tomorrow, or was it the next day—or the day after that?"

"None of them. I was to arrive next week, but I decided to come early, for a change."

Justin sat down on a chair across from the women. Glancing at the tea tray, he quirked an eyebrow.

"And who is going to pour tea today?"

Megan sprang from the sofa, shooting the Earl a murderous look.

28

'I think I had better return to the kitchen. I am sure I am wanted there."

"Thank you, dear, for your help," Lady Augusta replied. We must have another session when Justin is not around. You know how men are. They can go around chasing after poor scared foxes, but cannot appreciate the finer arts."

A quick look of consternation passed between Megan and Justin, though neither openly questioned the flame-colored peony's claim to art. Megan meekly beat as hasty a retreat as possible. Justin watched her broodingly while Lady Augusta watched him pensively.

"Really, my dear," she said, choosing another thread and casting him an admonitory eye, "you needn't have frightened the poor girl."

"Frightened!" barked Justin. "That would be impossible."

"Why, of course you frightened her," Lady Augusta retorted. "Did you see how she scuttled away? She's new, you know. Now I don't want you to scare her away, for she knows an awful lot about petit point, and I see a marked improvement in my flower already. She's the only one around here that has the slightest knowledge about it, except me, that is. I intend to work with her again. There can be no harm in that. We are far in the country."

"Yes, Mother. I wouldn't think of arguing with you," Justin said, a current of fond amusement running through his voice. "But if she is to become your sewing companion, I wish you would procure her a dress that fits, instead of being twice her size."

"Is that why I didn't like that dress?" Lady Augusta said in dawning enlightenment. "I knew there was something wrong, for it was terribly ugly." She seemed

29

well pleased to have settled that worrisome question.

'Yes, but tell me, how is my favorite Lady?" diverted the Earl.

Lady Augusta, looking rather shrewdly at him for such a featherheaded lady, obediently rambled off into her many worries and diversions and recalcitrant threads.

Chapter Three

A Toast, Of Sorts

Megan felt out of charity with her grandfather as the day trod ponderously by, like an out-of-sorts rhinoceros. The morning had greeted Argyl Court's occupants with a growl of thunder and a deluge of rain that had continued to spew down all the day long.

The household staff had sunk into a fit of the dismals. Cook's cake would not rise. The butler, Crispins, declared that everything was much too dusty, though how he could see that in such gloom went beyond Megan's understanding.

Then the youngest housemaid dropped a fine vase and went into hysterics. Members of the staff immediately ranged sides as to the importance of the vase and the competence of the maid. By noontime, a full-scale battle raged: butler against housekeeper, footman against scullery maid.

Megan's muscles ached from the unaccustomed work. The monotony of her labors made her want to run from the house screaming. Such feelings were intensified by the knowledge that if she were at Linton

Manor she could have been cuddled up with a novel and a pound of bonbons, neither of which had she seen since entering service. She had always enjoyed those days; that, in her opinion, was the proper way to brave a storm.

Seeing the view from the back stairs depressed her. She decided that upon her return to Linton Manor, she would decree that servants need only perform the most necessary duties on inclement days such as this. It was that, or pray daily for clear skies.

It was now ten o'clock, and all the servants had taken their squabbles and headaches to bed. Megan remained restless. She thought she would just putter down to the kitchen and get some milk. As a maid, she had learned to enjoy the kitchen. There always seemed to be something going on there.

"It really is the coziest room in the house," Megan declared out loud.

Walking into the kitchen, she spied Mrs. Bodkins still straightening up the room. The crackling fire reflected off the scrubbed copper boilers. The room basked in a warm, iridescent glow. Steamers, stockpots, and saucepans ranged the shelves, their lustrous sheen reflecting a myriad of tiny flames. Rough, amber-hued beams traversed the ceiling, and quarry tiles paved the floor, emitting a toasty warmth beneath her steps. The pungent scents of fresh parsley, thyme, and tarragon settled comfortably upon the cozy quarters, spiced by the fragrant scarlet geraniums along the deep windowsill.

"Ah, there you are, dearie! Still up?" Mrs. Bodkins asked unnecessarily. Bless her soul, thought Megan, she had sailed through the day with her usual good humor. She now faced Megan with unruffled composure.

"Yes, I don't seem to be able to settle down to sleep. I thought some milk might soothe me," Megan explained.

"Aye, today was rather stormy, both above the roof and below. What a tempest in a teapot! By the by, I was just settin' to carry a bottle to the Earl. He seems in a rare takin.' Just between you and me, dearie, he's already partook." She shook her head despairingly. "Somethin's a bothering' me poor Master Justin."

Megan almost spilt the milk. She could not envision the six feet of male arrogance for whom she worked as "poor Master Justin." Yet that was what he was to Mrs. Bodkins and that was what he would always be. If nothing else remained constant, old retainers would. A surge of warmth for the kindly housekeeper rose within Megan.

"Why don't I just take the bottle up to the Earl," Megan offered impulsively. "It would be no problem— I'll just deliver it and then go to my room. You shouldn't have to climb those stairs at this time of night." Megan's room was a snug little cubbyhole tucked back in the labyrinth of halls and closets between the kitchen and the main house. Mrs. Bodkins had said the room would be much handier, and there would be no need to crowd the rest of the staff in their quarters.

Mrs. Bodkins smiled at Megan in appreciation. She was such a thoughtful young lady. "Would you do that for me, lass? That would leave only a few things to be done here, and I can rest in me much longed for bed." The housekeeper knew she shouldn't permit it, but she couldn't refuse—the warmth of her bed called to her weary bones. Mr. Tothwell would be none too pleased, but it was certainly harmless enough for Megan to run the errand. Master Justin was such a gentleman.

Megan set the glass of milk and the bottle of brandy on the etched silver tray and climbed the stairs to the

Earl's room. She wondered what was bothering him. Somehow, it was comforting to know that he had had as dull a day of it as she had had. She wasn't being malicious—just a champion of equal justice.

What sort of mood would he be in this time, she wondered. He certainly was a volatile gentleman.

Justin propped his Hessians upon his desk and leaned back, waiting impatiently for Mrs. Bodkins to bring his brandy. He wouldn't put it past her to neglect to bring it, she being such a temperate soul. She had appeared so grim and disapproving when he had tendered his request. "And she being Irish," the Earl mused.

Couldn't a man be allowed to imbibe in his own home? What a deucedly rotten day it had been. At dinner he had not finished his first course when his mother tackled her dearest beloved subject, his sad lack of companion and spouse. She had not taken kindly to his gentle reminder that he did indeed have a companion—a certain widow with charm, but without innocence.

Ignoring that, Lady Augusta had continued to bemoan his lonely bachelorhood. It was time, she declared, for him to settle down. More importantly, it was time he set up his nursery. She was an old lady who despaired of ever seeing her grandchild. Didn't he care that the great Devenish name might die out? She delivered this in a sad, vague way; Justin knew she was at her most determined when she was her vaguest.

Uncle Josepheth then stuck his oar in the water, entering the inquisition with glee. It was a deed that must be done, he boomed. Duty had its duty. Justin should find a good-looking gel, one of those diamonds of the first water, get leg-shackled, beget his heir, and then go his jolly way. At this an elbow jabbed Justin's side roughly—might as well find a rich heiress while he was at it. A sly wink followed this. Uncle Josepheth wouldn't mind a few rich little Devenishes running about.

Justin pondered his uncle's and mother's arguments and sighed. They were right. He was thirty years of age; it was time he started thinking of setting up his nursery.

A timid knock at the door drew him from his heavy thoughts. Aaah! Here it was. Here was his brandy! Let his future wife and progeny be hanged!

"Come in, Mrs. Bodkins," he commanded quietly. The door swung open to frame Megan and her tray of spiritual sustenance. Candlelight enshrined her and she appeared a fetching angel, her uniform fitting her figure trimly for once. A well-developed figure at that, the Earl observed.

He pulled his muscular legs from the desk and towered over her. "So! It's not our Irish, tea-toting housekeeper, but our poker-wielding housemaid."

"Yes, my Lord. I told Mrs. Bodkins that I would bring your brandy. She was just straightening up downstairs." Megan couldn't decide why she was going into such inane detail.

Justin set the tray upon the tooled-leather surface of the table centered in front of the fireplace. Two large, burgundy brocade wing chairs were ensconced on either side; Megan looked appreciatively at the roomy, comfortable seats. Meanwhile, the Earl realized the presence of something other than brandy on the tray.

"My God! What is this?" The Earl wrinkled his nose as he held up the offending glass. Quick thoughts flew back to his nursery days—what was Mrs. Bodkins about?

"It's milk, my Lord," Megan said in surprise.

"Well, it certainly can't be for me," Justin growled.

35

"Or is it to be the chaser to my French brandy?"

"Oh no, my Lord. The milk is for me. I could not sleep—I thought it might help . . ., her voice faded. She felt a little foolish defending her milk while the Earl's brows arched higher and higher.

Suddenly Justin laughed. "So you've had a bad time of it also," he said knowingly. "Milk is not what you need to dispel the gloom of today, my dear. What you need is a generous glass of brandy."

He walked to the fireplace and poured the milk liberally over the burning logs. The flames sputtered and leapt up again in full force. "See. It has absolutely no purpose. Have a glass of brandy with me."

Megan, eyeing the fate of her unlucky milk and then his Lordship's glinting eyes, asked suspiciously, "Are you bosky, my Lord?"

"No, Meggy, just deucedly bored. I'd simply like some company." Weariness emanated from the man. Small lines etched his eyes. The lines decided Megan.

"Well—all right. I'll have a glass of brandy with you. A small glass, that is."

Justin sat down in one of the chairs and poured two liberal glasses. He quirked an eyebrow at Megan, who hustled over to the other chair and sank into the plush cushions. He handed Megan the now-murky brandy in the former milk glass; he certainly was not playing the gallant tonight.

As he leaned back in his chair, his cravat loose, his dark hair tousled, Megan thought of a conspiring schoolboy. This was a man you could easily befriend; she thought of the brother she never had. Without the company of her grandfather, Megan too needed someone to talk to on a rainy night.

The Earl raised his glass. "A toast," he proclaimed. "To relatives. God bless their interfering hearts!"

Megan hesitated—she didn't particularly desire to

toast all of Justin's relatives. Yet who was she to quibble? She thought of her grandfather and his dab of interference and she raised her glass in a fervent salute.

As Megan had never imbibed brandy before, she felt honor-bound to treat it like any other new experience—that is to say, with full enthusiasm and gusto. She drained the glass in a hearty swig.

Justin drew a sip, carefully eyeing Megan. A moment of silence ensued. Soon the salutary reactions Justin had so wickedly anticipated appeared. Megan's blue eyes shuddered and flew to Justin's in alarm. She attempted one desperate gulp and fell into a spate of coughs.

"Put your hands over your head," Justin cheerfully advised. Where he had learned such a muttonheaded piece of advice, he'd never know. Pulling himself from his chair, he walked over and thwacked her on the back in amiable concern. Megan, her throat burning, had the distinct feeling that the brandy had lodged in her chest instead of her stomach, where it belonged. Yes, she was certain it was trying to singe her lungs, if those organs still existed. Positive that her lungs had indeed been incinerated, Megan gasped a breath of a prayer.

Finally the coughing stopped, through no help of Justin. Glaring at him through teary eyes, she gave a hurt sniff and lowered her arms in embarrassment. Justin, unable to help himself, raised his glass. "Here. Wash it down with a glass of brandy."

The fire in Megan's throat blazed into her eyes. Her mouth, on its own volition, quirked and emitted an unladylike snort. The fact that it sounded more like a "snarrff" did not escape Justin's notice, and he chuckled.

"I guess you can't hold your drink. You had better stick to milk."

"I am perfectly all right," Megan retaliated in stung

37

pride. "It merely went down the wrong way." It detoured into my lungs, she finished silently. To support her declaration, she grabbed her milk glass defiantly, filled it, and took another gulp. It wasn't so bad that time, and she smiled in childish pride. "See!" she chortled.

"Yes, I see," Justin concurred seriously. He settled back with his drink. "Sooooo . . . Meg-the-poker, how do you like it here?"

"I don't like the weather," she grumbled, scowling.

"You couldn't have stated it better, my dear."

Eased by the brandy and the Earl's brotherly demeanor, Megan felt better. She listened to the rain for a moment, and thought, "Now this is the way to go on during inclement weather!"

"I'm not your 'dear', my Lord," she noted.

"And I don't like being 'my Lord'-ed. Call me Justin."

Megan knew how a lady would react, but was not sure how a servant should behave under these circumstances. This had been a niggling problem ever since she'd started her employment, for she knew that Linton Manor treated their servants differently than the outside world. Everyone, including the servants, told her this. Bereft of an example, she was constantly in a quandary. She hadn't known that servants sat about holding cozes with their employers on rainy nights. She rather thought that being a servant had its advantages.

Justin didn't know why he had given her leave to call him by his given name. He guessed it was her gamin grin, coupled with the enjoyable companionship that had sprung up between them. She certainly was the most different drinking chum he'd ever had.

He watched the severe concentration and transparent ideas that played across her countenance. He decided that this was an enjoyable pastime.

Megan took a considering sip of brandy and nodded at him, eyes now unclouded.

"All right . . . Justin. But only when there is no one around. Servants aren't supposed to call their lords by name."

"Oh?"

Megan smiled. The brandy was tasting better with each glass, and Justin was constantly refilling hers. He was a gentleman after all!

"And you must call me Meggy, not 'my dear.' You know how we servants gossip backstairs."

"Yes, by George. Faster than we above stairs. I will call you plain Meggy."

"Justin, this is a nice way to spend a stormy night. Even nicer than reading a book."

Justin grinned wolfishly. "I can show you an even better way to spend a stormy night."

Megan tensed warily. The first fumes of brandy were evaporating, and Megan, healthy girl that she was, started reclaiming lucidity.

Justin, honored at the club as a "six-bottle man," was also lucid. Recognizing her unrest, he said, "But, let us talk about something else. Do you know I have a very fine stable?"

"Oh, yes!" Megan exclaimed. "Some regular prime blood. Do tell me about it."

Meggy was a bang-up drinking partner, Justin thought again. Knows all about horses. Off they went into an intricate discussion of the finer points of horses.

Just when the Earl was concluding his account of his racehorse's last feat, he realized they had polished off the bottle. "Meggy," he announced somberly, "we're out of brandy."

"Should I get us another one, Justin?" Megan offered happily.

"No, no. Let me get it this time." Justin waved her offer aside as if he were swatting flies. He slowly pushed himself out of his chair and walked over to the door. He turned to explain. "If I am caught wandering about in the cellar at this hour, it is comme il faut. But if you were caught, it would not be the thing. Might cause all sorts of nasty suspicions. Might think you were having an assignation with the groom, what?"

Megan sprang from her chair. "You, my Lord, have a very bad sense of humor."

"I know, Meg," drifted back to her as the door closed. Blissfully content, Megan snuggled back and surveyed Justin's room again. She liked it.

Done in dark panelling, it held heavy, comfortable furnishings, all angles and lines. Her tastes in decor normally ran to the light colors and silks, yet a part of her felt an inherent liking for this room. It was so relaxing, so male. Her eyes strayed to the massive four-poster bed. It fit him. It certainly looked comfortable— Megan quickly directed her thoughts elsewhere, for she had a well-trained mind. The Earl returned to find her lounging in her chair, legs sprawled out in front.

"Here we are," Justin said congenially. "I'm so glad I went. You wouldn't have liked the stairs. Never realized how steep they were," he teased.

"I could have managed them. I'm sober as a judge," Megan boasted, eyeing not one, but two bottles cradled in the Earl's arms.

"Yes, I noticed that," Justin said. Amazed, he had, for Megan handled the brandy well, with only a slight slur in her speech and seemingly none in her thoughts. Remarkable!

He plunked the bottles down on the table with a clatter. One tipped over, rolling toward the edge, but Megan lunged and caught it. She sat back, clutching the bottle to her. Justin popped open the remaining

40

bottle and poured liberally. He might as well keep up with her in the spirits.

"Well, Meggy, why don't you tell me which of the young swains you have set your maidenly heart upon," Justin said as he quaffed his drink. Megan's eyes lit up—Not for nothing had Mr. Tothwell drilled her in her story. The challenge stared her in the face, and the brandy eased the lie. Her bemused mind latched onto the subject with relish. "I'm in love with Jed," she said expansively, attempting a soulful look.

"Yes, I know." The Earl was intent on his next sip.

"How do you know?" Megan was suddenly set off her stride.

"My valet told me," Justin confessed, shamefaced.

"Listening to backstairs gossip, Justin? Tsk, tsk. . . ." Megan tsked right into her next brandy.

"Yes, I learned it from an impertinent upstairs maid," Justin grinned. "What's he look like?"

"Who, your valet?" Megan asked in confusion, still concentrating on the busybody servant. "How should I know? Really, Justin, you should know—he is your personal man." It seemed appalling he could so inconsiderately forget his valet.

"No, no, your groom," Justin persisted fuzzily.

"Whose groom?"

"Jed!"

"Isn't he your groom now?" Megan was still quite in the dark.

"How—does—Jed—look?" Justin growled. Megan sat a moment, nonplussed.

"Oh . . . he's big." Belatedly, she remembered her lotharios's features. "With broad shoulders." Her arms flew out; the brandy bottle remained glued to one hand.

She likes broad shoulders, Justin thought distractedly. "That's all?"

"Hm? Uhuh."

Justin leaned on the table and peered at Megan. His thoughts travelled onward. Megan leaned forward and waited, for Justin seemed to her to be in the throes of some taxing idea.

"Meggy, I want you to tell me seriously," he pronounced intently, "who I should marry."

Megan digested the question. "That's easy. The one you love, silly." She giggled.

"But I don't love anybody," Justin replied, shaking his head mournfully.

It was Megan's turn to look puzzled. She thought a second. "Then you needn't marry anyone." She smiled happily, well pleased to have settled the question.

"Yes I do," the Earl persisted doggedly. "Mother says I do. She wants grandchildren: 'Lots of little noble Devenishes running about the hall.' It's my demmed duty . . . the sad fate of all good men."

"I see," Megan observed wisely, wagging her head to and fro. After a minute of such activity, she stopped. "What you do, then, is make a list of ladies that you could ask to marry you." She destroyed her sage pose by giggling again. This could be rollicking good fun.

Justin stared in awe. "That's a good idea, Meggy."

"First, think what kind of wife you want." Like a general, Megan began marshalling their errant thoughts.

"Oh, any old type. As long as she's no clinging vine, expecting me to do the pretty all the time."

"Don't you want her to be beautiful?" Megan asked in surprise.

The Earl considered it. "Nope. I've got a mistress for that."

"I know. Malissa Rambington. Most expensive widow." Megan paused as the Earl spluttered his drink.

"You shouldn't know things like that!"

"You've said that before; but I can, you know. I'm a servant," she reminded him proudly.

"Oh, yes." He calmed. They nursed drinks from the third bottle in quiet companionship.

"What about Milly Lambert? She comes from good blood, and her father is warm in the pocket." Megan rolled the unladylike expression on her tongue, relishing it. Being a servant did have its advantages.

"Yes, that's the ticket! Might as well marry an heiress and get some rhino out of it. Now we've got the right of it, I'll look only for heiresses—but not Milly Lambert. The chit giggles and blushes if you half so much as look at her. I'd strangle her within the fortnight."

"It's not her fault. She's supposed to act that way, she's a debutante," Megan said, as if it explained everything, which it did.

"Well, she's too young for me!" Justin stuck stoutly to his guns.

"Honoria Milligan. She's old enough."

"Not that old! She's an ape leader. I'd have to pry her off the shelf to get her down the aisle. Besides," he added in disgust, "she's platter faced."

'Thought you said you didn't mind if the girl wasn't pretty."

"Doesn't mean she has to look like a blasted turbot just landed."

"Sheila Tarrinton!" Megan was sure of this one.

"What? That ice queen? I want to go my way after the wedding, not before. That woman doesn't have a warm bone in her body."

Deflated, Megan concentrated, her blue eyes slightly crossed from the exertion. "But you have a mistress for that."

The Earl delivered a quelling stare, the effect only somewhat diminished by the bleariness of his eyes. "That won't fudge. Think of another one."

Megan turned severe, sipping her brandy for inspiration. "Uhh . . . Clare Brandon."

Justin thought a minute, perhaps two. Neither conversationalist noticed. Clare was pretty, well-behaved, and comfortably wealthy. "Why didn't I think of her before?"

Megan felt this was rather shabby since she had thought of Clare after much effort. She would prove that she was still the major thinker of the pair. "Or Blanche Shellingham."

The Earl snapped up the bait. "Yes, she would do nicely. She's got nice. . . ." He stopped short and looked at Megan, who was eyeing him darkly. He shook his head to clear it. "Ah, she's also well-endowed. Has nice . . . brown eyes," he finished lamely.

Megan wasn't deceived, and her eyes narrowed acordingly. So that's what he liked, did he? She didn't feel that Blanche was that much more endowed than herself, but if she was, it was indecorously obvious due to the plummeting necklines she favored. "How about Dimmity Childers?" she asked sweetly.

"Megan, you are a wonder. She's another one. Don't much like her father, but that don't signify."

"Certainly not. She'd probably not like your uncle," Megan offered with even more sugar.

"That's three likely candidates. Got any more?" Justin reached for the bottle that Megan clasped so lovingly to her breasts. She observed him foggily, focused on his outstretched hand, and then looked down at her chest.

Suddenly realizing what he was reaching for, she pushed the bottle into his open hand, blushing furiously. "No, I've thought of all three. It's your turn to think."

"All right, Miss Smart Servant, I will." Justin smiled cockily, pouring the next libations unsteadily. "I shall marry . . . hm, yes . . . I shall marry. . . ." He held Megan's attention by pointing a determined finger at her. "I shall marry . . . I shall marry . . . Megan Linton! That's who I shall marry," he exclaimed in a show of inspiration. Megan spluttered, choked on a burning swallow, and dashed her drink over the surrounding area.

"Now look what you've done. Thought you said you could handle this stuff?" Justin chided.

"Where did—where did you hear about Megan Linton? You don't know her," Megan whispered painfully through her tightened throat.

"Of course I don't, gudgeon. Just heard of her. Nobody's seen her, but she's full of the rhino. Grandfather died a few months ago. Ton's wondering if she'll ever appear on the mart, or stay a recluse like her grandsire—they say he was queer as a dicky-bird." Justin gazed at Megan with sincere, bloodshot eyes. "Should I marry her, Meggy? She has plenty enough blunt to satisfy Uncle. Maybe she'd even like to stay in the country and I could stay in town."

Brandy could have curious effects, Megan decided. An iron band pressed at her chest, shooting pain into her numb limbs while her eyes blinked rapidly from the salt of her tears. "No, I don't think you'll like her."

"Why not? Do you know her?" his voice held all the interest a soused man could muster.

"Well . . . a cousin of mine worked for her. Marrying her would be like . . . marrying me," Megan said with a weak smile.

"Oh." Justin nodded his head, though he didn't understand what she said. When he thought of it, Meg wasn't a bad sort; why would he not like this Linton woman if they were alike? Perhaps she meant that she was common. If so, that wouldn't do.

The mental processes of the brandy-impaired are

somewhat slow; while the Earl pondered, Megan had time to pull her scattered wits together. Watching him woozily, she prayed he would find another subject.

The Earl's thoughts did indeed find their own little tangent to follow. "Meg, you ain't so common. You're educated and speak well. Damn, you speak better than some ladies. And you said you read. Been thinkin' about that."

Megan stared. A spectral Mr. Tothwell sat beside the lounging Earl. "M—my m—mother was a good, respectable woman," she uttered in a monotone. She had to stop to remember words. Justin watched in concern; poor girl, he was hurting her with his careless questions. "My father was an aristocrat who played her false. I—I was born on the wrong side of the blanket. I n—never saw my father." She was trying very hard to think.

"Why, that bastard!" The Earl's snarl startled Megan.

"No, no you've got it wrong! He wasn't! He was of aristocratic descent. It's me that was . . . were . . . am!"

The Earl gazed at her blankly. He took another long drink, hoping for clarification. Megan drew a deep breath, then her eyes lit up. She remembered the rest. "My mother was a good companion to a f—fine, charitable lady. The lady, feeling sorry for my mother and me, allowed me to be raised with her children. This is where I learned all my accomplishments." Megan said it all very rapidly, before she could forget Mr. Tothwell's storyline.

"What happened next? Why did you leave them?" Immersed in her sad plight, Justin's natural cynicism was well-drowned.

"The older son took a liking to me. It was . . . necessary to leave." Megan looked down in embarrassment at telling such a rasper. It was such gothic drivel. Yet

46

Justin only saw the downcast eyes.

"The swine," he slurred, casting frantically about in his mind for a topic that would divert her sad thoughts. His spirit-logged brain, roiling, played him false, and he heard himself asking, "Would you like to dance?" Evidently his mind had decided that was a phrase you could safely ask a woman. Realizing what he had said, Justin looked suspiciously at his glass and determinedly set it down.

Megan stirred in surprise. Then the now-tipsy, mischievous imp residing within her giggled and said, "Why, certainly, my Lord." She stood up, teetering, and flourished a bow.

Justin pushed himself out of his chair and, following complementary etiquette, curtsied. He quickly understood why Megan had chosen to bow. It was by far the easier act to perform when skunked. "Shall we waltz, my dear? The music is divine."

Megan traipsed into his arms with a delighted giggle. His arms tightened and he swung her in wide circles, providing the music with a baritone hum. Megan gazed up into his eyes, hers suddenly wide. His every move guided her. Twirling and pirouetting, they did miraculously well for two dancers drunk as wheelbarrows.

"You are divine," she sighed dreamily, her gamin grin flashing across her face. Her wide grin and soulful eyes undermined his concentration and he stumbled over her feet.

Megan exclaimed and Justin cursed as they toppled ignobly. As fate would have it, they were waltzing beside the bed and both were surprised at the soft landing—the Earl even more so since he fell directly on Megan. His landing, he thought, was extremely soft.

Megan, who took the full impact of the fall and the Earl's weight, lost her breath sharply. Yet the tall, lean body pinning her seemed, amazingly enough, to be of a

47

comfortable weight. In fact, she magnanimously decided not to complain. For one thing, she did not possess the breath, and, in league with her body, her mind was not churning up one decent thought.

Justin, who had not heard an utterance from Megan after the fall, tightened his hold, seeking to peer into her face now conveniently close to his. "Are you all right?" he asked. Her eyes were closed and her head slightly turned from him. Suddenly the classic beauty of her features struck him. This, along with her gentle, clean scent—not at all like the average housemaid's—and the lithe, fulsome body in his arms conspired against him. He silenced the quiet "Yes" upon her lips with a kiss.

Megan, at first startled, relaxed under the subtle pressure of Justin's gentle, inquiring kiss. Never having been kissed like this, her first reactions were intriguing. She set her hand upon Justin's shoulders, desiring to steady her dizzy head, only to let her fingers splay across the rippling muscles she felt beneath his lawn shirt. Was this why broad shoulders had always attracted her?

Justin's kiss became more demanding, more probing. Without realizing it, Megan met the kiss with an open, exploring passion of her own. The slight taste of brandy upon lips and tongue only enhanced the moment.

She stretched in Justin's arms, reaching to enfold him. He clasped her tighter, moulding her body to his length. Her passion went to his head in a way brandy never could. Unfortunately—or fortunately—combined with the brandy, the effect proved overpowering. He sunk his head into her silken hair, now loosened and tumbled, and murmured, "Can't do this, you're just a kitten. Have to marry an . . . heiress." And he promptly passed out.

48

Megan lay dazed, willing the unknown sensations coursing through her to subside. She might be bosky, but she had a fair idea Justin had passed out. Rolling him over, she struggled up. Swaying, she gazed at him groggily. "Shot the cat."

She grabbed his booted legs and swung them onto the bed, bending his body into a rather awkward L-shape. She was much too dizzy to correct this, though, for the bed spun crazily before her, and she couldn't seem to catch him on the revolutions. Turning away from the whirling sight, she meandered, serpent-fashion, out of the room and to the stairs.

Megan blanched. A disembodied voice taunted: "You won't like the stairs, they are very steep." Oh yes, indeedy, they were very steep. She'd give her servant's pay, plus her Linton fortune, just to not have to descend those stairs. A nightmarish vision of herself lying in a muddled heap to be discovered by Crispins at daybreak spun through her head. What would Justin say?

"Never mind that, old girl," Megan advised herself sternly. "Just put one foot in front of another and you'll be safe in your little bed before no time." Only she couldn't find her feet, and when she did, she had grave difficulty budging them.

"That's funny," she whispered to the chandelier that hung over the abyss. "I learned to walk when I was just a small tot."

After dire concentration that made her swallow sickly, she enlisted her deadened feet in successfully reaching the bannister, to which she clung lovingly. Patting the smooth wood, she murmured, "Now stairs took me a little longer—not that I was a slow child." She leaned weakly over the polished bar and lifted her feet. The incline reached out, seducing her, pulling her down, feet thumping at each passing step.

"Whee!" Megan wheezed as her sliding ride gained compelling momentum. All too soon, she swooshed off the end rail, bumped to the floor, and whacked her head resoundingly on the newel post. Stars flitted about her head and the floor heaved beneath her. "Confound it, quit that!" she pleaded. As things settled again, she dusted her hands off, crawled to all fours, then jackknifed, derriere first, into an upright position. Arms outstretched and batting futilely at the darkness, she wandered drunkenly to her room.

Words careened in her head and she felt decidedly peaked as she crawled to her thin bed. The Earl's face circled before her eyes. A stab of pain followed. No wonder ladies don't drink brandy, she thought as she drifted off into a deep stupor.

Chapter Four

The Scheme Is Set In Motion

Megan groaned. Her eyes fluttered open swiftly, and closed just as swiftly. She groaned again.

Beserk hammers pounded at her skull. Fuzz lined the inside of her mouth and her tongue was nonexistent. She couldn't think what was the matter.

Then, regrettably, she remembered. Her conscience added its own throb. "Megan Linton," it accused, "you were foxed last night. Ape-drunk." Megan winced as she thought of those two bottles.

"The Earl helped," she explained to her woozy conscience. It was no good. She was at fault. She had not only drank, but carried on salacious, cant-infested conversation with her employer. That not being enough, she had cavorted across the room with a drunk—and she had kissed that drunk!

Worse, she had enjoyed that kiss. It had been wonderful—if one didn't mind earthquakes and fireworks at the same time.

That, however, was where honesty stopped in its tracks; she would not even consider what might have

51

happened if the Earl hadn't passed out so fortuitously. She was sure she would have slapped him like any properly reared lady—wouldn't she?

Most likely she had stayed her hand because she had never been kissed before and she hadn't been prepared for the explosion of feeling. So she explained it to herself. She wondered if kissing was always like that. Most likely it was—or perhaps it had merely been brandy-proofed. That was it! That demon brew was at fault!

Megan sat up, cringing. She looked down and suddenly realized she still wore her dress of last night.

She sighed. What a pity she couldn't wear it today. She must change, though, unless she wished to appear a vagabond waif rather than an upstairs maid.

She arose shakily and dressed by feel, closing her eyes tightly against the waves of nausea that rolled in with every movement. Finally, she braved her reflection in the mirror, and wished she hadn't. Anyone could have mistaken her for a runaway shade from the underworld.

Slowly, with the greatest of horror, her eyes focused upon an ugly purple bruise over her eye. What the devil! Where did that come from?

Moaning, Megan remembered. Confound those stairs, anyway!

Megan took a deep breath, reeled once, and manfully started her pilgrimage to the kitchen. Words of explanation swirled within her mind, flitting out of grasp.

"Ah, there you are, lass." It seemed Mrs. Bodkins was talking excessively loud this morning. "Ye're a little late—my God, child, what has happened? Ye look frightful!" she exclaimed with booming intensity. "Are ye ailing?"

"Oh, it—it is nothing, really," Megan stammered,

52

paling. "Just—just a headache from the storm. I didn't sleep well last night."

"Ah, 'tis a pity. That can fash a person. And didn't it thunder!" Mrs. Bodkin suddenly peered at Megan and gasped. "What happened to yer eye, lass?"

Megan's hand flew guiltily to the bepurpled spot. "I—I accidentally hit it on a door yesterday. Such a clunch . . . my hands were full at the time."

"Oh, dinna worry yerself. You'll be catchin' the way of it all. Soon armloads and doors will be the easiest thing. Just lucky ye didn't drop anything. Do ye want anything for that head of yours?" She was gushing with concern, for Megan seemed to be turning greener and greener.

"No. no. I'll be right as a trivet soon, you'll see," Megan assured Mrs. Bodkins in a sinking voice, for she didn't believe she would ever feel all right.

'That's just what Master Justin said this morning. He's a little under the weather himself, ye know."

"Is he?" Megan inquired weakly.

"But his ailment has nothing to do with the weather," Mrs. Bodkins whispered. "He's got a hangover."

"Does he?" Megan's voice was even weaker than before.

"Yes, deary, and if I say it, it serves him right. I found two more bottles of brandy gone this morn. That means he drank three, not counting that at dinner. Jug-bitten for sure" she pronounced disapprovingly.

"Three bottles!" exclaimed Megan. "Are you sure it wasn't just two?"

"Three bottles, lass! I don't care what ye say, there must be a bit of the Irish in me laddie." Mrs. Bodkins blasphemed the Devenish name proudly as she pushed a steaming bowl into Megan's hands. "Go and serve this to Master Justin before it loses its heat."

Megan looked down into the dish and blanched.

53

Kidneys! Why did it have to be kidneys? Her stomach churned, her head buzzed, and she gasped. "Sh—shouldn't there be a cover for this?"

"Yes, ye're catchin' on fine, dearie." Mrs. Bodkins picked up a silver cover and capped the offending sight. Megan sighed in relief. She offered a watery smile, turned, and walked stiffly toward the breakfast room. Stopping outside the door she gulped, afraid to face the Earl. Perhaps he wouldn't remember last night. Perhaps it could be blanked from his memory. Oh, if only it had been blanked from hers.

She pushed the door open nervously. Crispins, the pompous, thin-faced butler, stood ramrod-straight at one end of the table, awaiting orders. At the other end of the table, his master was the converse of Crispins. Though his beige and brown riding habit was sartorial, the face above it was shadowed with stubble, the eyes bloodshot.

The Earl glanced up from the newspaper that he halfheartedly studied. He held his head in the same fashion as Megan, as if an ant crawling across the carpet would be too noisome. The Earl studied her for one slow moment, inevitably focusing upon the telltale bruise over Megan's eye. Megan's initial embarrassment turned into a miffed simmer. Certainly he had no right to quiz her!

"Meggy, is that a bruise upon your brow?" Justin drawled.

"Yes, my Lord," Megan replied stoically as she curtsied. She felt decidedly ill. Crispins remained stiff, but his interest was palpable.

"Wherever did you acquire such a shiner?" Justin asked with studied concern.

"I hit it on a door, my Lord," Megan said through clenched teeth.

"A door, you say?"

54

"Yes, my Lord, a door."

"How unfortunate. You must be more careful. Ah—doors can be very dangerous."

"Yes, my Lord." Megan swallowed, eyes cast down. She flicked a glance over to Crispins, who remained a frozen sentinel, except for his eyes, which darted back and forth between master and maid with great suspicion.

Megan smiled quickly, with exaggerated diffidence, and glided over to the Earl, setting her burden down in front of him. In one fluid movement she removed the cover with a flourish. "Your kidneys, my Lord." Justin looked at the savory dish and froze.

"You she-devil," Justin gulped with deadly calm. "Take those away this instance."

"Yes, my Lord," Megan replied in a hurt, bewildered voice. Satisfied, she swiftly covered the dish, the sight of which still had dire effects upon her own system. As she turned to leave, Justin uttered a command. "I will be in my study, Meggy. Be pleased to bring me tea." She offered a stifled assent and made good her escape.

Fifteen minutes later Megan carried a laden tray into the Earl's study. Both winced as she set it down on the desk with a clatter. He glanced up from the correspondence in his hands. "The stairs?" he asked, nodding toward her brow. Evidently he had forgiven her for the kidneys

"Yes, they are dreadfully steep," Megan said, grateful for the reprieve. "All six hundred of them."

"There are only twenty-nine." The Earl smiled.

"There were more last night."

"Most likely. You must watch these old houses, my dear. They can be particularly playful at night. Change just like that!" Justin snapped his fingers, causing both of them to wince.

"Lawks, my Lord, and there being a full moon last

55

night," Megan whispered in an awed country burr, crossing herself quickly.

Justin laughed. "And it's Justin." He gave her a direct look.

Megan had no difficulty understanding his comment; she might have been suffering from an excess of brandy last night, but she was not daft. Last night flashed through her mind and she was at a loss for words.

She clasped her hands together and looked down upon them with deepest interest. It was much safer than looking into Justin's laughing eyes. Little did she know, but a telling blush betrayed her dilemma.

Justin watched with something akin to awe as he caught Megan in girlish confusion, something very rare and unexpected. Justin's friends would have been amazed to see the gentle light that crept into his eyes. He looked down at the letter before him and said with offhand aplomb, "I know I was foxed, but I do remember having settled the name issue. Though I'm not sure I remember much of anything else."

"You don't?" Megan blurted with budding hope.

"No, I don't." He thought of the heady kisses he had tasted before his mind had clouded over.

"What exactly do you remember?"

"Why, not much, I am sad to say. I seem to remember asking you to dance—definitely in my altitudes, it seems. But from there on, my mind fails me. Did we dance?"

"Yes," Megan admitted tentatively.

"Oh, I see. Strange I can't remember. I certainly hope I didn't do anything that might have embarrassed either you or me."

"Oh, no . . . no!"

"How fortunate," the Earl mumbled into his letter.

Megan sighed in patent relief. So over-relieved was she that she didn't catch the quick, knowing grin on Justin's face.

"Did you—ah—experience any physical discomfort last night?" Justin asked suddenly.

"Of course not," scoffed Megan. "Why? Should I have?"

"No, certainly not," smiled the Earl.

"Though I do have a devilish head today," Megan confessed. Now that she felt comfortable again, she did not mind admitting that. She remembered Mrs. Bodkins' orders to dust the downstairs and she pulled a duster from her deep side pocket, brandishing it in front of Justin. "May I?"

Justin blinked, unsure of where it had come from or what she intended. "Certainly, please do."

Megan promptly feathered the nearest chair. She performed this in a graceful but slow motion, grimacing only slightly. Justin watched and smiled. "It is common to experience a headache after one has enjoyed a goodly amount of brandy," he said. "You did well to handle three bottles."

"Thank you, Justin." Megan attacked another chair.

"And I didn't say or do anything that was not pleasing?" he asked intently, a slight smile upon his lips.

"Oh no." She gave an extra flourish to the highboy. "Though we did jabber a lot of make-believe., You probably don't remember, but we had a grand discussion upon marriage. We even drew up a list of eligible women for you. What a grand game it was. You know, I did enjoy the evening."

"I'm glad you did. So did I." Justin smiled absently. "Though that was not make-believe, Meggy. Sooner or later, I'm going to have to marry—I might as well get on with it. That list of ladies will do fine. I really had no

57

notion how to go on until you showed me the way. I'll simply survey them all. If you have any more information about them, please tell me."

Megan looked up from her last effort, a fine oak table. "You must be bamming me!"

"My dear, your language never ceases to amaze me. No, I am not 'bamming' you. It is time I marry, and all four ladies are eligible."

"All four?"

"Yes. Blanche Shellingham, Clare Brandon, Dimmity Childers, and Megan Linton. Have you forgotten?

"No, I haven't forgotten," Megan said after a stifled moment. "But do you have a tender for any of them?"

"Of course not. I've already explained that. I have only seen them in passing."

"It is to be a marriage de convenience, then?" Megan was still unable to believe him. She attacked a highboy with added furor.

"That is exactly what it is to be. I told you, I don't even know the ladies yet!"

"Lucky ladies!" Megan said under her breath. Justin cast her a dark glance.

"I see you are never more sensible than when drunk."

Drunk! Megan took exception to that, ready to inform him that it was not she who had been so castaway as to have passed out when he cut her short.

"What did you expect?" Justin could not explain why he felt so defensive.

"I don't know, something better! I expected you to marry for love!"

"Love! Meggy, that is for your class." Justin laughed and relaxed back into his chair. "The higher orders have simply admitted that there is no such thing as marrying for love. People marry for security and dependency. Or for money and position. It's truly safer

58

to marry for money and position. So many less illusions."

"Oh?" Megan pretended to dust.

"Yes. When people marry for that security they call love, they only end up making chains to shackle both of them. Chains, I might add, that no human should ever have to wear."

"That's only when you marry for security and not love!"

"Ah, Meggy, Meggy, I've seen supposed love matches. My God! The constant fighting, jealousies, and cruel games. From what I've seen, if there is such a thing as love, it cannot last a lifetime. The happy, besotted couple wake up one morning to find that what they thought they would find in their marriage and their love isn't there, and the disillusionment is bitter. They usually end up destroying each other, all in the name of love!" Justin's speech ended on a whimsical note, though it had been chillingly passionless.

Megan stood rooted, her duster limp at her side, her eyes pools of sadness. She pulled in a long breath.

"Poppycock," she said. "There is such a thing as love." She walked over and sat down without thought in the chair in front of him. "I've seen it and I've known it. And if it has happened once, then it must be. I know you'll say those are accidents, or those people are very lucky—"

"Or are very competent liars."

"There you are out! That's the problem. Love needs honesty. Honesty to the other person, and more importantly, honesty to oneself."

"Ah, but honesty hurts so."

"So does dishonesty. And the pain from dishonesty sometimes lasts longer. People do things in the name of love that have nothing to do with love—that's when you start making those chains to wear. The jealousies

59

and games are not part of love, they are the weaker, childish parts of us that come with love. I don't want to say that people purposely lie—"

"I'm so glad."

"But people get confused on what kind of love they're feeling, or what need it's filling—loneliness, insecurity, or passion. You marry when you find the full love, not the one that takes care of just one or two of those needs. It's the love where you care more for the other person than yourself and he cares the same for you. Then love won't destroy—it will build!" Megan took a long breath and pulled back in embarrassment. Philosophy was not the best topic for two people suffering from severe hangovers. Arising, she sped to the half-dusted shelves and started feathering determinedly.

"Oh Meggy, what a romantic you are. And what happens if you never find that love? You don't get married?" Justin leaned back in his chair, watching her. Somehow, he couldn't let the subject end.

"Yes!" Megan replied. Justin chuckled and she said hotly, "It's better than marrying without love and having a marriage like you talk about. A marriage of convenience where you're a fake!"

"A fake? Isn't that a bit harsh, Meggy?"

"No, it isn't." She felt angered by his baiting. "Sharing your life and children with someone you don't love belies what marriage means. That life leads to marital wrecks or that search for fulfillment that our—your—society condones, which is taking a long line of lovers. And what if you meet the one you really love, do you make her your mistress also? Just add her to the list, since you married beforehand?"

Something twisted inside him at that. Staring at her flushed face, he didn't know what to say. Deep down, part of him thought of love. His parents had loved each other in their unique way; perhaps that was why he had remained unmarried. Yet he was getting older—the world-weary part of him didn't believe anymore. Meggy seemed an innocent romantic. He sighed. "Meggy, my air dreamer, let us cry a truce. I will let you marry the way you choose, and you will let me marry the way I choose."

"Certainly, my Lord," Megan offered with deceptive meekness.

"Dammit, Meg! I am at the ripe old age of thirty, and it is time to marry. According to Uncle Josepheth we can use some more money, though God only knows why, and Mother says she can use some grandchildren—again, God only knows why. I assure you, Meg, I have had many loves and I haven't met one that I would want to spend my life with."

"All right, then," Megan said bitingly, "which of these fine fillies do you wish to choose? And you can count Megan Linton out," she added angrily.

"Out? Why?"

"Because—because—I hear she's common, and wants a love match!" Megan suddenly wished she could kick herself.

Justin was astonished. "You servants are amazing. Such gossips. But I'll keep her on the list, nevertheless. We shouldn't listen to gossip—it might surprise you to find even the most romantic of ladies might settle for what I offer."

"Don't be so cynical!"

"It's very hard for me not to be. It is a bad habit of mine," he apologized. "Now, let us stop wrangling and decide how I am to set about choosing a bride."

"Why not write a questionnaire and have all the ladies answer it?" Megan suggested sarcastically. She deepened her voice. "How much is your dowry? Do you talk at breakfast? Do you snore?"

"That might suffice." The Earl was enjoying Megan's rising anger.

"Or better yet, you should have them all line up at Tattersills so that you can inspect them properly and get the highest offer from their fathers. I'd suggest you have a doctor present to guarantee they are healthy brood mares. And above all, don't forget to inspect their teeth!"

"That's it, Meggy!"

"What?"

"I shall bring them all together. I'll throw a house party which will allow me to look them over."

Megan merely gaped. Unused to the way of the ton, she thought him a stark raving lunatic; that, or he was still frightfully in his altitudes. "Just why do you think these incomparables would drop their routs and balls to come travelling here, simply so that you can show your gall by inspecting them like so much horseflesh. You'll have to go to Almack's—they certainly won't come here at this time of season."

"Meggy, Meggy, where have you been? They'll come. I'm one of the finest catches of the season. In fact, I'm a matrimonial prize!"

"You're an egotistical boor is what you are!" Her head throbbed and her temper boiled. She shook her duster in severe agitation until—after all the aggravation of the morning—it gave up the ghost and scattered feathers in all directions.

Megan sneezed. Justin, watching the feathers float lazily to the floor, smiled wickedly. "We will most definitely have a party. Perhaps even a ball, with the local gentry."

"Yes, my Lord. May I be dismissed?" Megan ground out.

"Anything you wish, Meggy."

Megan slammed out of the room. She growled as she

heard Justin's laughter through the closed door.

Justin held firm and the gears of Argyle Court whirred and coughed into mechanization. Megan sighed, trying to imagine how Lady Augusta had entertained before her arrival. Fantasies of demented servants running madly about, royalty and peasants rooming together, and major catastrophes occurring every hour on the half-hour, were what came to mind. Naturally, this would transpire while Lady Augusta floated benignly by, taking tea and stitching.

Megan was present this year, thanks to her grandfather's quirk, and it seemed that she and Mrs. Bodkins might creditably scrape by. Megan had organized Lady Augusta's ten dozen conflicting orders and the servants were once again gaining confidence after a siege of panic. The rooms were aired and readied. The great hall and ballroom shone with beeswax and polish. An agenda blazoned itself within each servant's head.

Megan, sitting in the yellow room, grimaced as she ran her eyes over the list of those who had responded. Justin would crow that they had all accepted—except for Megan Linton, she thought spitefully.

She and Justin had not held conversation since that last battle. If passing in the hall, he was cool, far removed from the inviting man of before, while she could not help but be quiet. Frost edged his orders and her "Yes, my Lords" were stilted. Megan wondered if he was still in temper, or if she had finally overstepped the boundaries and he would never again treat her as anything but an insignificant maid. Which would suit her fine, she thought sternly. Any closeness was dangerous to her masquerade and useless to her life.

She smiled. He certainly had been right in this case. Every woman on their list had been embarrassingly prompt in response. Well, if these silly widgeons would come flocking to his imperious summons, they deserved whatever shabby plot he had in mind.

Admittedly, if one was shopping for a helpmete, Justin would make a fine figure for a husband. He would be an experienced . . . Megan's mind skittered away from such thoughts. He would make a fine husband, if one liked that arrogant type.

The door cracked open, and the object of those featherheaded damsels' dreams, the noble cliff that drew those beribboned lemmings to Argyle Court, peered in. "Silly widgeons," Megan muttered under her breath.

"I beg your pardon. Were you talking to me?" Justin surveyed her with an impassive stare that had Megan wishing she had studied up on jungle cats.

"No, my Lord, I was just talking to myself." She looked down at her paper quickly.

"Talking to yourself already? I see the strain of preparation has been too much for you." Crossing to her, Justin bent over her shoulder and read the list. Megan stiffened; removing her hands from the paper, she tightly clasped them in her lap. Justin stood as casually as possible, trying to focus on the letters in front of him. He felt as if he had walked into a charged zone and his muscles tensed against his will. He studied the straight, prim figure. Damn, why did he feel this way? Why should this servant's censure bother him? Why did he even allow her temper? "I see that Clare Brandon has accepted."

"Yes, my Lord."

And so did Blanche Shellingham."

"Yes, my Lord."

"And so did Dimmity Childers."

"Yes, my Lord—and so did Malissa Rambington." Megan said it without missing a beat or changing a tone.

"As I see," Justin said stiffly. "Did not Megan Linton accept?"

"No, my Lord . . . she was out of the country." Megan's eyes were fixed upon the list.

'That explains her absence," Justin answered, expecting, nay, hoping, for a reaction. Megan maintained the same, irritating poise. Frustrated, he wanted to take those straight, sturdy shoulders and shake them until the primness and tension were gone. Even more, he wanted her to look at him. Perhaps then he could break this self-conscious spell that crackled and fizzled about them.

Instead, he put his fingers under her chin and gently tugged so that she must look at him. Ignoring the shock waves that coursed through her, Megan followed his silent request and looked up at him.

Justin's finger traced the smooth white skin along her jawline. "Am I still in your black books?" he asked. There was no arrogance, only gentleness.

"No, I thought you were still hipped at me," Megan said in surprise.

Justin's face lit up and he laughed in relief. Never mind why; Megan was interesting and he did not like it when she was cool. They were on safe, friendly territory again.

Megan laughed easily, feeling the tension drain from them both. She pulled her jaw from his fingers and nipped them.

"Ouch!" Justin said on an arrested laugh.

"Serves you right. I hope you end up riveted to one of these girls. I hope she shrewishly keeps you under the cat's paw."

"And snores atrociously. If I do, I'll elevate you to lady's maid so that you may suffer with me."

"You'll do no such thing! I won't be there." Justin did not have time to ponder this remark, for the door opened to frame a well-groomed head.

"Hallo, there," said a light baritone. A slim, elegant body dressed to the nines in blue Weston jacket and high, starched cravat, joined the head.

"Edward, what are you doing here?" Justin exclaimed in a stern voice. Megan wondered who this young man was to draw Justin's censure.

"I heard you were having a party and decided to visit?" Edward offered in a hopeful tone.

"Why are you here?"

"Well, you see, I was sent down again. It wasn't all my fault, but I'll tell you later. Wouldn't want to discuss these matters before a lady." Edward tipped his beaver hat with an engaging grin to Megan.

"This is not lady, this is Meg!"

"No lady? Why, Justin! And you brought her here, with Mother? Not the thing old boy, not the thing."

"She is not my mistress," Justin said forbiddingly. "She's a housemaid in employ here and you had better remember that." Justin smiled at Megan. "She's already taken after Uncle with a poker."

"Ah, so you have met the old duffer," Edward said to Megan. "A likable dinosaur, what?"

"Most definitely," twinkled Megan. "Now that he has become so circumspect with me."

"Uncle has taken to skidding around corners and hiding under tables when Meggy is in sight," Justin informed Edward.

"Oh, is that who I saw hiding in the suit of armor when I came? I thought it was Crispins inspecting for dust."

Megan gave a deep, throaty laugh. She definitely liked this scamp. Justin tried to quell her with a stern eye; Edward grinned at her. "I say, I like you, but what are you and Justin doing in here?" He looked at the papers. "Dictating billet-doux, Justin? You really should make him do that himself, ma'am," he advised

Megan kindly.

"Meggy is checking the guest list for the house party to make sure it is in order."

"What is the maid doing that for? That should be Mother's duty."

"Do you really think she should?" Justin's brow quirked.

"Lord no, if Meggy can do it, it is definitely better. Can't forget the last party where Mother put Lord Darlington with Lady Stanford in one room, and Lord Stanford and Lady Darlington in another. That was how the real sleeping arrangements were, you know, as Mama had heard from all the on-dits. So Mama connected them together in her mind, regardless of marriage titles, and housed them that way. Thing is, they all came at separate times and it wasn't discovered till night—Lord, what bustle. They acted outraged, of course, and we switched them around properly—just so they could sneak about and intrigue for the next week. But mother had them scared there for a while— almost ruined all the fun for them. She is such a bufflehead at times. I keep thinking there must be a sense of humor there, but it didn't look like that—just pure absentmindedness." Edward shook his head sadly. "Oh well, who have we invited for this week?"

"Not we, young cawker—you will not be here."

"Now let's not get hasty, Justin." Edward scanned the list over Megan's shoulder. "Brandon, Shellingham—who are they? Don't know them. Childers— know the father. He's a crony of Josepheth's, Meggy. Better keep your poker polished. Usually he's too drunk to be of harm, though. Ends up hugging the potted palms, waiters, musicians—bad eyesight, that. Well, party sounds slightly flat—ah! Much better! Malissa Rambington! Now I know her!"

"Edward," warned Justin in a deep growl.

"Don't know her as well as Justin, of course. Only stands to reason." By this time, Megan was quivering with stifled laughter. Justin put a restraining hand on her shoulder.

"Trenton Pavnor!" Edward looked up in consternation. "Why are you inviting that rum touch?"

Megan studied Justin with interest. Lady Augusta had also reacted strongly to that name, even more strongly than to Malissa's. To Malissa's she had fluttered an "Oh, dear," but to Pavnor's she had clucked loudly and jabbed fiercely at her peony, which, under Megan's direction, was slowly obtaining horticultural classification. Justin's face was shuttered as he replied.

"I have my reasons. Now, I think it is time we had our discussion, Edward."

"Knew it was coming. Had to open my mouth. Had to ask the wrong question. Will you protect me, Meggy?" Edward's pitch rose in feigned alarm.

"You can't hide behind my skirts," Megan vowed with a merry eye.

"But it certainly would be much more fun than the bear-jawing I'll get from Justin. He cuts up devilishly stiff, you know." Edward winked and lowered his voice seductively. Megan could see the resemblance between the brothers. Did Lady Augusta know that her youngest son was a scapegrace and her eldest a rake?

The door swung open again and, lo and behold, Uncle Josepheth appeared. "Yoicks! Edward, my boy, thought I heard you. Come here and give your old uncle a hug." Edward obliged him, though Josepheth barely reached his shoulder. "So you were sent down, were you? Over some petticoat, I'd wager." Josepheth winked slyly at Edward. "Ahhh, you've got my blood in you, you young rascal. You haven't seen your mother yet, either, I bet. Will she be in a taking! She'll have

68

your head for washing." He ignored the fact that Lady Augusta was rarely in a taking over anything except her stitching.

Stopping to breathe, he saw Megan. His face reddened and he grabbed Edward, pushing him out the door. "Here, you sly young dog. Le's go to another room." Edward looked back in perplexity and shrugged.

"I'll come with you," Justin called after them and followed.

"Edward, beware that chit in there. Touched in the upper works, daft. Why, attacked me with a poker. . . ."

Looking after the men, Megan thought once again what a strange family they were. They certainly were an assorted menagerie, but a merry lot all the same.

Chapter Five

Masks and Facades

There remained one inhabitant of Argyle Court, and solely one, who was not longingly gazing with dizzy anticipation toward the forthcoming house party. Excitement pervaded the air, yet poor Megan did not enter into those high flights. Indeed, she dreaded the affair. No small wonder, since she ran every danger of discovery as a sham with such a host of nobles about. The frightful possibilities were enough to cause even a female as stout as Megan to become vaporish.

She did, however, place some small hope in the fact that she did not personally know any of the invited guests. She had ensured that when she aided Lady Augusta with the invitations.

The most imposing challenge lay in her ability to not draw the nobles' attention. One could not say that her past record stood her in good stead, but perhaps her luck with those not derived from the Devenish tree would be better. She could only try her utmost, for it would be very lowering to later visit London (after she had gained her fortune and escaped her servitude) only to be singled out as the Earl of Argyle's upstairs maid.

She then smiled with deep pleasure. She might surely dread the threatening house party, but she fully intended to enjoy its primary event, the masquerade ball. Fate, strangely enough, had been kind to her there.

She and Lady Augusta had been diligently working on a wilting leaf that was slowly taking the shape of a cucumber, despite Megan's strongest efforts, when Lady Augusta had petitioned her for ideas on entertainment for their visitors. Megan applied her mind to the matter, and inspiration had struck. If she suggested a masquerade ball, perhaps she could watch, masquerading herself. Without considering a moment more, she presented the idea to Lady Augusta.

Unfortunately, Lady Augusta did not approve the idea, complaining that masquerades often degenerated into sad romps. Unable to let her idea fade, Megan swiftly agreed, but then suggested that they revise the theme and have a Moonlight Masque.

What was a Moonlight Masque? Why, proper ball attire would be required, but everyone must be masked, servants included. Imagine how few preparations would be needed, yet the decorations could still be haunting and romantic.

"My dear, what a clever idea." Lady Augusta added yet another growth to her leaf. "For it is the masks that intrigue one. Eyes look infinitely delightful behind masks, don't you agree? Though I can't fathom why. There is something very oppressive in the thought that humans look best when hidden behind masks. But as for costumes! Well! I cannot imagine anything more wearying or uncomfortable. One is always clutching and grabbing at it, simply to protect decorum. Otherwise, one is forever tripping over the costume—or worse yet, others. Gracefulness cannot be hoped for.

71

I remember I was forced to dance with a knight once. Dreadfully uncomfortable, my dear. And dangerous! I was positive at every turn that his sword would run me through. Yes, we'll not have costumes, only masks! And plenty of candlelight! We older women always show to advantage in candlelight!"

Megan chuckled in remembrance as she passed through the upper hall, saluting the austere knight that stood sentinel duty there. Hearing a commotion in the downstairs hall and knowing that guests were soon to arrive, she quietly sliped into the shadows. Once again the ancient warrior offered protection as she peeked past him in curiousity.

A knock resounded through the hall. Crispins swiftly appeared and opened the door with his accustomed pomp.

A stack of bandboxes with two legs entered. The legs soon proved to be owned by a footman who tilted inward. Three more footmen, equally burdened, staggered after. Lastly, a china doll with golden ringlets and eyes of cornflower blue traipsed delicately forward; garbed in a powder blue travelling dress, she carried an enormous muff.

The muff squirmed and emitted a ferocious bark. "Now Pewwy, stop squaming," admonished a clear, adorably childish voice. "Mamma wants you to behave, Pwecious."

Crispins, after one frozen stare, bowed with a polite mumble and crept away. Megan whistled silently, giving the child due credit for routing him so effortlessly where so many more imposing figures had failed miserably.

Suddenly, a babble of voices pierced the air, the most raucous fighting to the top. "Damn, Madame, I only

72

grazed your carriage by a hair. I drive to an inch. It was your driver! A more ham-fisted hacker I've never seen!"

A tall, thin man burst wildly through the door. His fine white hair srayed outward and his goatee stood on end like a disturbed porcupine. Light blue fish-eyes watered over a red, bulbous nose and he was quivering and trembling, his long limbs twitching. Dusting himself off righteously, he spun around, raising an emphatic bony finger.

Not a word did he utter, for a fulminating matron sailed forward at full mast, ruthlessly cutting him short. Under purple bombazine, her plump bosom heaved in accusation.

"I'll have you know, Sirrah, that my man is one of the finest drivers. A Brandon would have nothing less. If not for his superb skills, we would all be lying dead in a ditch! You, sir, were driving like a madman! Oh, I am so overset, I feel a swoon coming on!"

Megan smiled knowingly. That intrepid beldame would not care to faint while so enthused with her high dudgeon. Evidently the thin man was not as perceptive, for he eyed her suspiciously. "Damn, Madame, don't drop here! There's no space for such goings-on. Dimmity's got it all cluttered with her bloody bandboxes."

The matron took extreme exception to such heartless advice and moaned zestfully. "Oh, you cruel man! Clare, quickly! My hartshorn!"

A willowy redhead dressed in the kick of fashion wafted to her from behind. Her shapely hands gripped a wadded handkerchief, a vinaigrette, and hartshorn. Nervously handing her mother the hartshorn, she clutched the vinaigrette to her own nose.

The enraged matron, with a face now as purple as her bombazine, sniffed long and deeply from the bottle.

73

Much revived, she shook it violently at the man. "Sir, I beg you not to use such—such—language in the presence of these dear innocents. My girl Clare is of a fine, delicate temperament. She is a true artist with great sensibilities."

"Dammit! What did I say?" Lord Childers demanded in total bewilderment. Dimmity, one of the young innocents whose ears he supposedly sullied, cast Lady Brandon an equally baffled look. Clare, knowing how offended her great sensibilities were, raised a trembling hand to her clear hazel eyes. "Oh, Mother," she whispered, "I fear this is too, too much. I feel I will faint."

"Damn, doesn't anybody listen! I just explained to your mother we ain't got room for you!"

Suddenly, a new voice was heard—Dimmity's muff sprang to life and yapped his objections. Both mother and daughter screamed and clutched at each other, their vials rattling, and one handkerchief escaping to the floor. "Eeeek!" Lady Brandon screeched. "Take that wretched mongrel away from here!"

"He's not a wwetched mongwel. He's a pedigwee poodle named Pewwy," Dimmity lisped sweetly. She pushed the snapping beast forward in open friendship.

"Pewwy?" Clare asked, wide-eyed. She was almost stunned out of her oncoming faint.

"Yes. I named him Pewwy 'cause he is a Fwench poodle," Dimmity explained. Her cornflower eyes shone in pride at her own cleverness.

"French!" Lady Brandon looked at Perry in renewed horror. "All the more dangerous! Take that foreign monster away!" She shrieked as Perry upheld his nation's honor by snapping her one remaining handkerchief from her hands and worrying it mercilessly. Then, looking her dead in the eye, he dropped it rudely to the floor to join its mate. "Out, you cur!"

74

Dimmity gazed at her in hurt bewilderment, still proffering the growling Perry. Mother and daughter, fearful eyes glued to the snarling "Pwecious," backed away. "Sire, did you hear me?" Lady Brandon half-bellowed. "Take your daughter's dog away!"

During this social interlude, Lord Childers—wisely leaving the field to Dimmity and Perry—had backed away and sat upon one of the trunks, sneaking a reviving swig from a silver flask. Lady Brandon's bellow snapped him to attention and sent him toppling from his perch. "Ahh—what did you say?"

"May I welcome you to Argyle Court?" A cool, deep voice spoke before Lord Childers could receive the retribution he had so witlessly invited down upon his head. Justin walked nonchalantly over to the brangling aristocrats, stopped, and offered them a gentle smile, the picture of lordly elegance.

Lord Childers scrambled to his feet, whipping his flask behind him. Something was heard to splash on the marble floor. Dimmity swirled around with a sweet, welcoming smile upon her rosebud lips.

Clare quickly unclutched her mother and stood with downcast eyes, a maidenly blush becomingly painting her cheeks. Lady Brandon inhaled her anger and posed herself with a stately turn. As for Perry, he ceased his French barking and returned meekly to his prior muff's position within Dimmity's arms.

Justin was about to begin his welcoming speech to the now-benign party when a flash of movement from the stairs commanded his eye. He turned in time to glimpse Megan flitting away through the shadows. A slight giggle floated downward. Pressing his lips sternly together, he turned and greeted his waiting guests.

*   *   *

75

Adjusting her mask snugly, Megan adroitly lifted a tray of champagne glasses. She turned from the serving centre, which was cunningly hidden behind trellised screens. In front of them, an impressive display of lobster patties and other delicacies rested upon over-bedecked tables. Masked maids circulated amongst the elegant throng.

The ballroom shimmered in candlelight. The guests glittered with jewels and rustled in fine silks. Ravishing and rakish in masks of rainbow shades, they spun to the music, a kaleidescope of colors.

Megan surveyed the noble crowd, well-pleased. So far, all had passed without a setback. Her eyes roved the room, studying and identifying various people. Edward, she noted, in a red mask was making an elegant leg to a shy squire's daughter. Lady Augusta, the Devenish sapphires blazing upon her throat, was happily, if haphazardly, matching and mixing young couples. Megan stifled a giggle as she watched the numbed, dismayed looks upon the young people's faces. Capricious Cupid would need to look to his laurels with Lady Augusta applying her hand to the business.

A pink dress with five white flounces drew Megan's attention. Ah! Dimmity! and the listing man with mask askew over his nose must be Dimmity's papa, Lord Childers. Stationed near the punch bowl, he nevertheless lunged at the champagne glasses that unfortunate maids carried by.

Megan's eyes continued restlessly across the room, stopping when they fell upon the seventh Earl of Argyle. He was attired all in black with only fine white lace at the cuffs to lighten the severity, his black mask serving to add the final devilish touch. From under lidded lashes, she studied his tall frame. Her gaze reached his face and she started.

Justin, his eyes fixed upon her, sent her a quizzing look. He tilted his head slightly, signalling her to come to him.

Attempting to be inconspicuous, she bobbed and curtsied, offering champagne politely, until she stood before him. "How did you recognize me?" she whispered, very worried. She looked around furtively, then remembering, demurely offered him champagne.

Justin grinned. He could recognize her fluid movements and lithe walk in any crowd. "This is not a full masquerade; why shouldn't I recognize you? Surely you recognize others here tonight?"

"Why yes, my Lord, you have a full covey of possible pigeons here!"

"Now that's the proper spirit." Justin applauded quietly as he nodded to a passing baron. "Which one of the marks—ah, young ladies, should I approach first?"

"You mean stalk, don't you?" Megan suggested dryly. "Why not Dimmity? She is such a sweet, comfortable child, she should suit you perfectly."

Justin merely looked down his nose at her. "And where is she?"

"Over there, by the squire's son."

"Oh, the strawberry confection? Yes! Well, I'm off. I'll dance with her first, and then the other ladies in succession. That is the fair and decent way to go about it, don't you think?"

"My Lord, I dare not say what I think at this time. I'd always heard you aristocrats were a barmy lot, and you are. Go court your pigeons, I must serve champagne." Megan curtsied smartly and moved away.

A slight, amused smile played aross Justin's lips at her open disapproval. He watched as she bent to serve a drink. She possessed a controlled energy not found in a lady of leisure, nor in an awkward peasant—where had she acquired it? Not a woman in the room rivalled her in grace, yet he remembered well the taut, well-toned body she hid beneath that drab dress. At that, Justin sternly shook his thoughts away, bringing his mind back to the business at hand. He spied Dimmity across the room and walked over to ask her to dance. She fluttered her eyes and giggled . . . and giggled.

Fans flew up to matron's faces as Justin and Dimmity joined their set, for they were a stunning couple, Dimmity's golden curls just reaching Justin's shoulder. Determined not to watch the dance floor or the coldly calculating Earl, Megan offered drinks to a blustering squire and his wife. She successfully absorbed herself in her work until she heard Dimmity's voice close at hand as the music ended. "How vewwy stwong you are, my Lord. You must be top of the twees in evwything." Dimmity sounded amazed.

"Just as you are delightful in everything, Dimmity." Justin offered the words politely and excused himself. He walked over to Megan.

"One down." He took a glass from the tray and sipped deeply. Eyes on the floor, he asked, "Next?"

"Clare Brandon. Over there." Megan nodded quietly in the direction of the redhead dressed in sea-foam green. Justin nodded his head and crossed purposefully toward her.

Megan's tray was empty and she went willingly to replenish it. As she came away from the serving centre, she glimpsed the dance floor and Justin caught her eye. She quirked her head, shooting him a questioning look, as if to ask what he thought of Clare; he gave a slight shrug, then turned his gaze and smile back to Clare.

"I say, what sort of rig are you and Justin running?"

Megan jumped, setting the champagne sloshing within the glasses. Turning warily, she found Edward looking down at her, his eyes alight with curiosity.

"We are not running a rig. What makes you think that?"

"By all the smiling and nodding and looks passing between you. Too smokey by half, my dear."

"Are we that obvious?" Megan asked in alarm.

"No, only a needle-witted, observant, and totally brilliant brother like myself would have noticed," Edward conceded.

"Good! Hmmm—I assure you, it is nothing more than keeping in close contact to insure that everything runs smoothly this evening."

"I see you plan to bamboozle me," Edward moaned sadly. "Though I assure you, you are an excellent fabricator—something I have always admired in women. Well, perhaps you can tell me why Justin is dancing with females he has never looked at before?"

"Edward, they are all eligible ladies," Megan protested.

"Precisely. Zeus, who wants to dally with a clutch of eligible females? It's enough to sink a fellow. Now I have always preferred accessibility to eligibility."

"In other words, the muslin company," Megan snorted. "For shame, Edward, you have let your uncle sway you. I assure you that someday you will find the eligible female much more interesting."

"If by that you mean you think I'll be bacon-brained enough to make a misstep into parson's mousetrap, you are all about in the head. Zounds, Meggie, never say that Justin intends to turn Benedict."

Luckily for Megan, her mind had drifted during the inquiry. She cut Edward off abruptly with, "Who is that girl Justin is standing up with now?"

"That, Meggy," Edward chuckled, "is Blanche Shellingham. My mother forced me to dance with her before. Justin should be having a hard time of it now. You should have heard our discussion—indecorous!

The girl wouldn't let off telling me about her favorite mare that was about to foal. Now is that a proper thing to discuss with an unsuspecting stranger while on the dance floor?"

"She might have thought congratulations were in order."

"Perhaps. I must remember to send her a box of cigars for the happy occasion." Edward reached for a glass of champagne.

"Don't be so hard on her. And that is the second glass of champagne you've taken from my tray."

"Meggy, you are sounding very much like Mrs. Bodkins. I am merely helping ease your burden by taking them off your hands—or tray, rather. I'm certainly the innocent one. Look at old Childers over there, he's had two trays-full. You'd better watch him after the third—that's when he becomes playful."

"So you have informed me." Megan curtsied.

"Speak about playful, there's Malissa Rambington. Guess I'll go over and say hello."

"Huh!" Megan thought as she watched him stride toward the widow. Covertly, she studied the raven-haired beauty dressed in vibrant gold. Only a self-possessed woman of such beauty could have carried the creation off.

Not wishing to look upon the lady further, Megan searched for Justin in the crowd. He was politely returning Blanche to her chair. She was a rather pretty girl in a healthy, substantial way, with large brown eyes and chestnut hair; Megan could find no fault in her from where she stood, unless it was the sophisticated neckline that overtly displayed her rather ample charms. Yet when Justin turned from Blanche and caught Megan's gaze, he cast his eyes heavenward and shivered.

He shrugged his broad shoulders and smiled lazily;

Megan could tell he was in a dangerous mood. He walked deliberately over to Malissa and, after asking for her hand, threw Megan a well-satisfied look. It said, "Ah, here's the one."

Megan pulled a frown of feigned indignation. Before Justin could respond she turned and offered champagne to the nearest turbanned dowager.

Megan didn't feel particularly well. She had easily joined Edward in the jests over Justin's mistress, yet now that Malissa was here in the flesh—and such voluptuous flesh, at that—the jokes paled. Instinctively, Megan disliked the woman. Malissa reeked of calculation (not to mention cynicism, egotism, and blatant smugness). Grandfather was right, she decided fiercely. Men were indiscriminate fools where women were concerned. He had always said that given their choice of women, men would invariably jump to take the worst choice.

Well, Megan had had enough of serving for one evening. No one would notice if there was one less maid—she and Mrs. Bodkins had seen to that. The ballroom had grown quite warm and Megan decided that a breath of fresh air would revive her.

With only two lonely glasses left upon her tray, she hunted out Lord Childers and offered them to him with little compunction. Beaming at her through watery eyes, he grasped them gratefully, for the rest of the staff had sagely begun to avoid him. "Never can find a maid when I want one. Began to think you people were inhospitable. But knew that couldn't be," he whispered in drunken bewilderment.

Megan felt unaccountably better. Watch him topple into some dowager's lap. That would certainly liven up the party, she thought impishly.

She slid down the hall and into the library and sighed happily. No one would find her here, for the private anterooms generally drew the guests.

It clearly was not Megan's evening, for she had misjudged on two counts. She had erred in assuming no one would notice her departure, for someone had. Edward was not the only sharp-witted man to detect the constant passage of looks between master and servant. Trenton Pavnor had.

Indeed, Pavnor had been watching the Earl for the lion's share of the evening. When he noted the pretty serving maid's stealthy exit, he followed out of curiosity. He fully intended to know the game they were playing. This caused Megan's assumption that no one would discover her to go begging. She sunk deeper into her easy chair as a well-built man of medium height with silver-blonde hair stepped into the room.

"I saw you slip away." He finally located her through the shadows. "Now, what would a pretty little maid like you want to do, sitting here all alone. I'm not interrupting anything, am I?"

"No, you are not," Megan snapped. She didn't wish for company. No, wait—perhaps a light flirtation would tease her out of her brown study. For, inexplicably, her distracted mind had centered upon Justin's kiss on that rainy night. Did kissing anybody make one feel the way she had that night? It probably did, since people engaged in the practice so often and so indiscriminately.

An idea presented itself to her. Perhaps she should experiment a little and discover the effects of kissing a man other than Justin. She studied Trenton with a speculative eye. Here was a likely candidate who might oblige her. Needless to say, Megan's scientific logic far outstripped her wordly knowledge. She smiled in what she hoped was a flirtatious manner. "No indeed, sir. I simply came in here to escape the crush. Solitaire can be so lovely at times, don't you agree?" Megan arose

82

and drifted over to the fireplace; the man was too close, too imposing.

"I agree. But solitaire for two is an even more enjoyable game, don't you find?"

"I would agree with you, sir, but I don't believe I'm acquainted with it," Megan said lightly, wondering what the man could be talking about. Surely he didn't want to strike up a card match? She attempted a speaking glance from under half-closed lids for added measure. New to dalliance, she was unsure of the exact quantity of seductiveness required to prod a man to kiss.

Pavnor, looking into those half-lidded blue eyes, needed no more evidence to determine the game played between master and maid. Forsooth, it was one of the oldest in history.

Gad, but Justin had fine tastes. Perhaps that was what caused such blood rivalry between them, Trenton mused. Excitement coursed through him, for if Trenton could succeed with this little piece, this would not be the only woman's attention that he and Justin had vied over. He chuckled. Yes, he would beat the wealthy, high-and-mighty Earl of Argyle in more ways than one, someday, but for the present, there was a lovely armful smiling at him.

"Ah, I'm sure you have, my sweet, but nothing would give me greater pleasure than to—ah—refresh your memory." Smiling, Trenton stepped forward, took her in his arms, and bent to kiss her.

Megan stared in astonishment. She would never have guessed it as uncomplicated as all that to lure a man to kiss oneself. Yet, now that he was so obliging, Megan rather wished for a tad more resistance on his part, thus allowing a minute more for mental preparation on her part. Overset, but doggedly determined, she gave herself up to be kissed.

Nothing happened. There were no fireworks or volcanoes. Faith, not even a sizzle. In fact, she found she didn't particularly enjoy it and did not cherish a repeat.

Pavnor soon discovered that the body within his arms, albeit warm, was unresponsive. Seeking to deepen the kiss, he came up against primly pursed lips and barred white teeth. The siren of a moment ago had somehow metamorphosed into the stern governess of his youth. Picqued, and in sudden fear for his expertise, he urgently redoubled his efforts.

In one stunning moment he was torn away from her. "Trenton—I fear you overstep the bounds of our hospitality."

Megan had tightly closed her eyes in distaste; she opened them to discover Pavnor dangling like an errant puppy from Justin's outstretched arm. The man jerked free, seeking to arrange his crumpled jacket and pride, his fair complexion quite mottled. "Beg pardon, Justin. I did not know she was under your—protection. You always were a possessive sort, weren't you?"

"Trenton, strive to lift your mind from its natural habitat—that being the gutter. She is not what you think, but she is under my protection from the likes of you."

"And also from the likes of you? Now that I find hard to believe! You're a dog in the manger, Justin. You always were."

Anger burned and Justin's muscles tensed into cords. Megan was hunting for conciliatory words when a cool, musky voice broke in.

"Now, men. Let's not fight over this—" Malissa had entered the room. Her amber eyes raked Megan. "—this serving girl. Tonight is a festive occasion and I refuse to allow any disagreements or tiffs."

Stepping between the two men, she laid a possessive

hand upon Justin's arm. Megan sniffed before she could repress it. Her indignation grew as Justin laid his free hand intimately upon Malissa's and said evenly, "You are right, Malissa. Thank you for recalling me to my duty. Please take Trenton and offer him a drink; I wish to talk to this maid."

"Don't be too severe with her, darling," Malissa purred, kissing Justin and nodding at Megan maliciously. "Come along, Trenton, I do believe you have this dance."

"Exit Mistress Bountiful," Megan fumed as Malissa led Trenton away. She glanced at Justin. His eyes were burning-grey lava, his brows flaring like the wings of an enraged eagle. She repressed a cringe, shaking herself sternly; she refused to be cowed and treated like a disobedient child. Unwisely, she chose the offensive.

"I suppose you and Malissa required the room. I'm dreadfully sorry." She strove for a blasé voice.

"Malissa and I did not require the room," Justin ground out. "Edward mentioned that he had seen Pavnor follow after you, and knowing your penchant for attracting trouble, I came to assure myself of your safety. Evidently, you were very safe. I find it exceedingly strange that you saw fit to fend off poor old Uncle Josepheth and me, and yet you accepted that scoundrel. Faith, I guess there's no accounting for some people's tastes."

"I could say the same," Megan unthinkingly retorted.

"You go too far!" He caught Megan's arms in a painful grasp. "My God, your impudence knows no bounds! A mere servant and you act the duchess. I am fast losing all patience with you. Heed me, and heed me well: I will brook no more of your insolence. You have not only dared to question my actions but you deserted your post to dally with one of my guests. This I will

85

not allow!"

"You will not allow—! I admit you have a right to chastise me for dereliction of duty, and, yes, my impertinence in questioning your tastes. But what right do you have to question who I 'dally' with? Who I kiss is my affair. You do not command my life!" So spoke the Lady of Linton Manor, not a maid born and bred. Her independence shouted for expression; she'd be hanged if she'd tell him she was simply experimenting to understand the effects of his kiss.

"Now there you are out, my misbegotten wench," Justin said cruelly. "I do have command. If I choose, I can turn you out without a reference. You would never be able to find employment if I choose to use my position against you, so don't tempt me, you little fool!"

Sudden understanding of his dominance over her exploded in Megan's mind. The fate of a female servant with no references would be tragic. Lady Linton, though, could not capitulate. Her eyes narrowed to slits. "Fine! Toss me out, use your noble name against me, let me starve or better yet, let me become haymarket ware!"

"Oh no, Meggy, that would never do for you," Justin offered silkily. "You could do much better for yourself, I'm sure. I know some friends that would willingly set you up in 'proper' style."

Megan gasped. Her hand flew up in bitter retaliation, but Justin was quicker. He caught her fine-boned wrist in a punishing grip, sending pain stabbing through her arm. "Don't you ever dare to raise your hand to me!"

Megan blinked back sudden tears, lost to her shaking rage. Pulling in one ragged breath, she suddenly calmed herself. She faced Justin with muted, smouldering eyes. He held her stare.

With a strangely gentle motion, he lowered her arm. His hand held her throbbing wrist loosely for one remaining moment, then he was gone.

Megan stood tense and still, refusing the blurring tears. Dear God, she wished she could leave this place. But she wouldn't; her grandfather's will must be fulfilled. That, however, was not the overriding reason. Megan Linton, Viscountess of Marchington, would never run away from anything or anyone.

Chapter Six

Swords, Stables, And Surprises

Megan drew a long breath of scented morning air and surveyed the building before her. Built in the Grecian style, it was a gracious structure; she was amazed that the late Earl had spent so magnanimously on a fencing room. Mrs. Bodkins had revealed that the Earl had enjoyed fencing above all sports, spending hours in the room. Megan would have loved to have known him; as husband to Lady Augusta and father to Justin and Edward, he must have been an extraordinary man.

Megan, judiciously playing least-in-sight, had not seen any of them for the last three days. She had felt it incumbent upon her to inform Mrs. Bodkins of her small fall from grace, reporting that she had deserted her post and that the Earl had caught her in the dastardly act. She wisely neglected to mention that quite a few abusive words had been tossed about over the unfortunate discovery of her "experiment."

Mrs. Bodkins had shaken her head, clucking, but had taken things in stride. "Well, dearie, I should turn ye off, and that without a reference, too, but ye're a good lass, much too helpful to me in other ways than serving drinks. Best thing to do is to keep ye out of the way of Master Justin. He'll soon be forgettin' the whole botheration if ye don't remind him of it. So I advise ye to make yerself as scarce as hen's teeth for a wee while. I'll try and find ye jobs far out of his ken—but if ye lose hours, they'll have to cut into your days off."

"I can help in the kitchen," Megan offered eagerly. "Or collect some herbs. We're shockingly low on them."

"That's the right of it, lass." Mrs. Bodkins and the rest of the staff had already discovered that Megan was very helpful with the minor ailments and injuries that befell them.

Mrs. Bodkins had not found work for her today, and she was free. In her hunt for herbs, Megan had discovered that Argyle Court included a fascinating collection of buildings.

She pushed open the door and stopped, watching as an unbooted figure performed feints and parries in the air with a tipped foil. He made an overextended lunge and slipped. "Blast and damn!"

"For shame, Edward. Strive for a little control."

Edward jumped up and spun around, flourishing his foil. "Meggy! Tars and hounds, woman, you gave me a start! Don't you know better than to sneak up on a man when he's concentrating? You'll make me old before my time."

"You achieved that before you ever met me, scamp."

"You'd best not throw that at my head, shrew. There is an old saying about what the pot calls the kettle."

"Yes, and I've always wondered exactly what names it used. I gather from that obscure and very unflattering remark—pot, indeed—that you have heard some salacious remarks, no doubt made by your esteemed brother."

"If you mean ones on the order that you were caught in the library trading kisses with a loose screw rather than serving champagne like a good little maid, yes. Though I'd go bail that the latter was the more exciting of the two." He looked at Megan's glum face, speaking with friendly candor. "Gads, woman, why did you pick Pavnor as your partner in that peccadillo? Nothing could have been more sure to set Justin's back up."

"Peccadillo! Don't make it sound so disgraceful. You make it sound as if it were a flamboyant affair rather than one kiss. Why, Betty, our temporary downstairs maid, has a string of—of flirts. There is the squire's son, and John the footman, to name only two."

"John, you say?" Edward was interested; then he looked at her sternly. "Now hold it, my girl, you can't throw me off the scent so easily. We both know Betty is different from you—you could say she was born to that kind of life. She's up to all the rigs, and then some. Now you, on the other hand, weren't raised that way. It's plain as a pikestaff." Catching Megan's look of consternation, he added for good measure, "Even Betty has never been chawbrained enough to get caught kissing Pavnor in the library."

"How was I to know he was Trenton Pavnor? I assure you, I would not have kissed him had I known."

"That is why one generally asks a man his name before one bestows one's kiss. Bet even Betty does. It's not difficult at all, old girl, you simply say—," and he assumed a ladylike falsetto, fluttering his eyelashes madly, "'Excuse me sir, before I place my sweet, rosebud lips upon yours, may I have the honor of knowing your name, place of residence, and portion per year.' And if he is slimy enough to be Trenton Pavnor, you draw his cork. As simple as that!"

"As simple as that," Megan laughed. She pictured

herself landing Pavnor a facer. "I will remember that, though I fear I could never achieve such a wonderful effect as you did."

"Rather good at it, ain't I?" Edward concurred, grinning boyishly. Then he turned serious. "Cut line, Meggy. I'm still waiting for your answer. Why were you dallying with that dirty dish—I know you're not the type to play fast and loose. Trenton's the one you should have taken an armory of pokers to."

"Oh—I don't know why," Megan confessed dejectedly. "I'm not sure you could understand."

"Try me. You'll never find a more likable father confessor again."

"Or a more unlikely one," Megan smiled. She considered Edward's concerned face. "It's just that I was restless. I was curious about kissing."

"Ha! It's all this bucolic country air that degenerates a person. Look at Betty, she grew up on the stuff! It never happens in the city."

"It's all the degenerate people around, you mean—a girl can't carry her poker all the time. Alas, that a good maid like me could fall into such a decadent situation." Megan hoped her jokes would get her out of being quizzed further, but then he looked at her with a glimmer of understanding and she decided to try and explain fully. "It isn't fair. You men are allowed all the license you want, while we women aren't. How are we ever to understand how we feel if we don't experiment?"

"Experiment?" Edward yelped. "The lady kisses a man she doesn't even know the name of and calls it an experiment! Well, it was one of the most tottyheaded experiments I've ever heard. Zounds, Meg, you'd be sure to come a cropper with that one—dished quicker than a flea can jump a dog. You see, my green little goose, your partner might not have such scientific

91

thoughts on his little mind—I'd vow on my grand-father's grave that Pavnor didn't. Gad, Meg, I don't understand you. Didn't your mother teach you anything? I'd have thought she would after her experience." He caught Megan's questioning gleam and stuttered. "Now don't look that way at me—I ain't about to explain that to you. Why, it'd be dashed improper. But just trust me in this advice—never trust any man. Any man! There!"

"Now don't patronize me, Edward. I am older than you, three months at least. I'm sure I could have handled the situation if you hadn't sent up such a hue and cry after me. Now I've truly blotted my copybook."

"Ha, mine's stained beyond repair."

"So the wind sits in that direction? Justin's still cross as crabs? Whatever did you do to get sent down for so long?"

"Nothing that hasn't been done before."

"That should narrow it down. So there's still nothing new under the sun?"

"Let's just say that I was caught in one of my own experiments," Edward said ruefully.

"And that experiment was—"

"Whether a dancing bear will still dance in a dean's office," Edward grinned. "She will. Lord, you should have seen Hoffer's face. Unfortunately, the poor animal—the bear, that is—became instantly enamored of old Hoffer and took him to her—ah, bosom, as it were. You should have seen it, Meg! Dancing Rosie—that was her name—was pawing and hugging Hoffer as if she'd found her long-lost cub. Perhaps she had, come to think of it—that Hoffer is a queer old bird. Sad thing, though, for old Hoffer would have it that Rose was mauling him and smacked her on the snoz with a musty old tome—Sophocles, I think. Almost broke old Rosie's heart, he did."

Megan laughed. "Oh, dear. That's why you're hiding out here, practicing fencing rather than joining in on the fun and frolics of the enchanting company your brother is keeping."

"Enchanting is coming it a bit too strong, Meg. But yes, I'd rather avoid Justin's wrathful way at the moment—it won't hurt to practice my fencing, anyway."

In the short time she had observed Edward's swordplay, Megan had noticed a definite flair, but some of his movements definitely needed polish. Some of them were the very same ones, in fact, that her grandfather had tweaked her on many a time. However, she only smiled. "Oh no, I'm sure you're very good."

"I can't hold a candle to Justin. He was taught by my father; the old governor was a nonpareil. I only wish I was half as good."

Megan detected the wistful note in Edward's voice. She suddenly thought of the lonely childhood Edward must have had, worshipping the older brother who was always away and the father who had died when he was young. She hesitated, then said diffidently, "I know you will not credit this, but I was not as strictly—supervised—as other girls my age."

"I will credit it. Just been telling you that." Megan cast him a quelling look and continued.

"I managed to study some fencing with—the boys of the family we resided with. I'm—not very good, but—I certainly could help you practice the rudiments. I saw many passes that I would like to try a hand at."

Edward stared at her incredulously. Megan's heart sunk. Why must she do these impulsive things! But oh, how she missed the sport!

"Meggy . . . you are the queerest duck. Always full of surprises. Makes me wonder about you. Just can't

93

imagine your life before you came here. Know things no female ever knows, then don't know any of the things you ought." He eyed her almost sternly and Megan held her breath; then he smiled. "All right, Meggy. I'm not going to look a gift horse in the mouth. Since we are both fugitives from my brother's frown, we might as well not waste our time. We shall fence our way out of boredom, but don't be surprised if I trounce you. I'll give no quarter just because you are a woman."

"I wouldn't expect any," Megan said with a secret smile as she reached for a foil.

They spent a rousing half-hour at play. Megan thrilled at flexing her muscles and feeling cool steel within her grasp again. She subtly suggested improvements to Edward, crediting them to overheard instructions.

Soon she regretted the confines of her dress; as the practice continued, so did Edward. The result was an appointment to meet another day, when Megan could find different attire. The miscreants parted on excellent terms.

The dry, musty hay warmed Megan as she burrowed into it. She had heard voices outside the barn and had escaped to the hayloft. Now, secure in her straw fortress, she cocked her head to catch distinct voices.

Lord Justin and his guests rode into the barn. Drawing back, she thanked the almighty for her narrow escape; she would not have enjoyed discovery by her least favorite lord and his guests. She had hoped for some friendly gossip with Jed, since she was bored to flinders, and here she was, stuck up in a hayloft!

"I don't see why we have to stop riding just because Dimmity fell on her bum. She has no seat," Blanche accused in a gruff voice.

"It isn't my fault that howwid horsey thwew me off, is it, my Lord," Dimmity breathed soulfully to Justin.

Worming her way to the edge, Megan peered over carefully. Justin, Dimmity, Clare, Blanche, Malissa, and two nondescript gentlemen stood in conversation as the grooms came for their horses. "Well," she observed to herself, "the Sultan and his harem have arrived. The two ignored chaps must be the guardian eunuchs."

Dimmity's blue eyes were now swimming in pools of tears. Megan growled, perceiving that Dimmity was a member of that special breed of women that could cry buckets with narry a runny nose or reddened eye.

"Of course not." Justin, wearing a hunted expression, patted her arm.

"The wabbit cwossed poor Wambling Girl's path." Dimmity was evidently unconsoled. Megan wondered what strange urge prompted Dimmity to name her animals with r's. Perhaps she enjoyed the challenge.

"That doesn't mean you had to fall into a fit of hysterics," Blanche snorted. "You scared the horse more than the rabbit ever did."

'I think she acted as well as could be expected," Clare entoned in her gentle, musical voice. "She is not like some who lack all sensibility. Who are not even overset when strange men enter their boudoir in the still of the night."

"I suppose I should have cried and sniffed at my vinaigrette while some old roué ravished me?" Blanche retorted.

Arrested explanations swirled around her at this. Curiosity blossomed in Megan; this conversation alluded to the shrieks and noises she had heard last night. Unfortunately, for once being prudent, she had stayed in her room rather than risk running into some of the nobles in her night clothes. She had planned to

95

ask Jed about the night's events that morning.

Apparently Clare's finer nerves had taken exception to Blanche's plain speaking, for she passed one dazed hand across her brow. "Oh no," Megan breathed in alarm. The rest of the company, apparently just as well-trained to Clare's sign language, hastily stepped back, giving her a wide berth. Everyone except Dimmity. She placed her dainty slipper where all others feared to tread.

"Oh please, Clare. Don't swoon here. Think of your pwetty widing habit."

"I think we should all, perhaps, go to the house, where we may plan the upcoming picnic," Justin said quickly, before Clare could decide whether to hit Dimmity before the floor. Like condemned men set free, the noble group rushed to obey while Clare still debated. Finding herself deserted, she shook off her trance and followed, none too happily.

Megan waited impatiently, eager to find Jed and discover what had really transpired last night. Yet, as Malissa and Justin brought up the rear, Malissa detained him with one white hand upon his sleeve.

"That was a very interesting display." Her eyes gleamed at him. "But whyever did you invite these people here, darling?"

"I do not think that concerns you, Malissa. Let us just say that I desired different company for a variation."

"What, debs and innocents?" She was confident as only an experienced, beautiful woman could be. "Come, darling, they aren't in your style. They are quite droll, to be sure, but boring, nevertheless." She ran her hands over his chest, her eyes molten. "Don't think I do not see a design in this, but I can please you better than any of these dewy-eyed misses," she purred. Her arms twined around his neck.

"Blanche is no dewy-eyed miss," Megan wanted to shrill from her perch. Painfully, she swallowed the hot words, only to bite her tongue in shock as Justin pulled Malissa into a burning embrace. Pavnor's kiss had been a mere handshake compared to the clinch in which Justin held the woman.

Breaking away, Malissa laughed, sensuality in every pitch. "See, darling, we are right for each other in every way. Will you come to me tonight?" She nuzzled his ear. "I miss you so, Justin." Then she nipped at it. Good heavens, Megan thought, is that how it goes? Or is Malissa just cannibalistic?

Justin smiled slowly but noncommittally. "Perhaps."

Disbelief almost unbalanced Megan and she teetered on the loft's brink. She highly doubted that Justin, with his libertine propensities, hadn't already visited that lady's lair. If he hadn't, he most certainly would. A vision of him dressed in a silk smoking jacket, skulking down the hall armed with chilled champagne, and tapping suavely at Malissa's door filled Megan's mind (that being the most decadent picture she could imagine). Yes, she thought cynically, he most certainly would visit that black widow during her stay.

"Go and prepare for the picnic. I'll join you in a trice." Justin disentangled himself from Malissa.

"And what shall I wear, Justin darling?" she asked provocatively.

"Oh, anything. You look divine in whatever you deign to wear, my Aphrodite."

A giggle bubbled from Megan at such blatant flattery. If that was what one had to say to a mistress, she deemed it a mixed pleasure to mount one. She waited a few seconds, to be sure they had left, and proceeded to climb down, confident everyone had departed.

97

Justin had heard the muffled giggle. He walked two steps past the barn door, turned, and walked back. Treading silently, he viewed the pleasant sight of Megan backing down the ladder, skirts swaying and trim ankles showing. As she reached the last three rungs, Justin could contain himself no longer. "And just what do you think you are doing?"

The effects were unfortunate. Megan, intent on her humorous thoughts, was startled. She jumped, then grabbed convulsively for the rung, but her hand only contacted air. Still looking up, Justin received a hurtling body in his arms and they both shot backward.

Justin remembered falling with this exact same body in his arms once before. What was it about this woman that always spelt catastrophe for him? He grasped her tightly in aggravation as he hit the hard floor. "Dammit, Meggy, what do you think you are about? You've just ruined my coat," he complained, as he heard the poor garment rend.

Megan squeaked, rolled away, and bounded up in one fluid movement. It was as if he had the bubonic plague, Justin noted. Gasping, she shifted off one ankle. "I'm terribly sorry, Justin," she stuttered, red-faced. "You should not have sneaked up on me like that."

"So I perceive." He groaned his way to a vertical stance. "And feel," he added as he kneaded his back.

"Yes, my Lord—now I must leave," Meggy mumbled self-consciously. She hobbled away as fast as she could.

"Meg, you've hurt your foot," Justin said in concern. He hastened to her.

"I'm fine," Megan insisted, hobbling all the faster.

Ignoring the blatant untruth, Justin clasped her firmly by the shoulders and steered her gently over to a bale of hay. "As I don't see. Stop hopping about and sit down. Let me have a look at that ankle."

"No, I'm fine!"

Justin stared intently at her. She tried to relax. "I'll look at my own ankle, if you don't mind. I know a little about doctoring."

"Coward," smiled Justin.

"That's better than being Aphrodite," Megan murmured. She rubbed her ankle, trying exceedingly hard to suppress a wayward smile.

'Ah, we have an eavesdropper in our midst," Justin confided to the barnyard cat that had come up to rub against his legs.

"When you are caught up in a loft there is very little to occupy your time," Megan said breezily, as if a hayloft was the commonest place to be in all the world. Her eyes were fastened on an ant struggling to overcome a piece of straw in front of her.

"And I suppose it was absolutely necessary to retreat to the loft?"

"It was that or a convent."

"Seeking to escape the wrath of man, Meggy? The hayloft is a novel way to go about it."

At a loss for words, Megan reached down and pushed away the straw that barred the ant's progress. As she did so, her sleeve slid up, betraying a fading bruise encircling her wrist. She jerked up quickly and pulled at her cuffs.

Seeing the movement, Justin caught her wrist and pushed back the sleeve. He traced the revealing mark gently with his thumb. Gazing at it, he said quietly, "I think we both have tempers and say things in the heat of them. I will apologize, if you will do so at the same time."

Megan's wrist trembled within his grasp. Unable to look away from those hands, she said in the same hushed tones, "On the count of three. One . . . two . . .

99

three. I'm sorry," she said at the same instant the Earl said, "I apologize." They looked at each other.

"Now that wasn't so difficult, was it?" Justin grinned. He had forgotten to unhand her wrists.

"No, though I can't understand why you were in such a pucker over my small indiscretion. It was a mere platitude—nothing like that which you offered Malissa." Megan tried not to sound piqued. She met Justin's warning gaze as his fingers imperceptibly tightened over her wrist. She hastily freed that ill-used member. "May I serve a change of subject, oh great Apollo, darrrling? What was all that commotion about last night?"

"You did not hear about it?" Justin's grey eyes glinted, the hazel flecks in them sharpening in amusement.

"No, I was up early and away."

"Touring the barn, no doubt." His face shaded, though his smile remained the same. "Perhaps it was a rendezvous with a certain groom, little one?"

Megan's eyes flew to his in shock. Rendezvous with a groom? Surely he could not believe such vile things of her? Justin read it as prevarication. "Change of subject, returned to you. I deeply regretted that you were not there last evening to partake of the entertainment—it was the unofficial social event of the season. Certainly it would have appealed to your unusual sense of humor. I can only assume that you sleep like the dead, for everyone else down to the tweeny came running. I had my eyes peeled for you, expecting at any moment to see you charge in, buttoned to the throat in a sturdy, wool nightgown—confess, that is what you wear— swinging your favorite poker with holy fervor."

"Such indecorous thoughts, Justin." Megan's attention had wandered elsewhere—darn this masquerade! She would have loved to have been there.

"Never fear, your poker was not required. Indeed, the lady in question did not require your or anyone's protection, including the good Lord's."

"A lady in question? I believe I begin to see the travelling hands of Uncle Josepheth."

"What a quick-witted girl you are! You are quite right. Our rampaging roué was on the prowl last night, except that having tippled so much, he apparently directed his amours to the wrong floor, the wrong room, and definitely the wrong woman. He had unwisely stumbled into a room to make love to . . ." Justin paused for effect as Megan's eyes widened in anticipation. "To none other than Blanche Shellingham."

"But how fabulous!" Megan exclaimed, clapping her hands together, waiting like a breathless child for his next words.

"Have you no heart, you wretched women? Just think of my poor, benighted uncle. Ah, but we Argyle men are made of sterner stuff—we stand up under fire. Fighting against the greatest odds, Uncle successfully made it across the room undetected, and with the finest homing sense found the bed—another of our special talents. Think of his utter consternation when he reached to cuddle what he thought was a willsome maid, and got his ears boxed roundly for it. Instead of a little slap and tickle, poor Uncle received nothing but clouts and curses."

"Curses?"

"Curses! Blanche sent up a screech of 'Rape!' Yes, my dear, that was the very word she shouted to the rooftops. Naturally, hearing this banshee cry of foul wrongdoing, we all rushed to her room, all in our various night attire, mind you—what a leveller that was in itself! You should have joined us, my dear. Mrs. Brandon was frightening in a puce creation. Lord

101

Brandon must hide under the bed all aquiver when she threatens to visit his room."

"Oh, dear—I fear to ask what Malissa Aphrodite was wearing." Megan considered that. "She was wearing something, wasn't she?"

"Never you mind. As I was saying before I was interrupted, by the time we arrived, the carnage was dreadful to behold. Uncle Josepheth had been toppled out of the bed and entrapped in the sheets, Blanche atop him, milling him mercilessly. Still crying rape, mind you. You could barely hear Uncle whimpering for all the din. And he accuses you, you know."

"Me! I wasn't even there—though I wish I had been."

"It seems you are a witch who cursed him. Nothing has been right since you took after him with that poker. Are you sure you did not achieve your aim? Perhaps you did not disclose all the details to me?"

"Odious man, of course I did," Megan blushed.

"Well, no fear of you toad-eating me, is there, my dear? But let me continue . . . here was Blanche, abusing Uncle heartlessly, and we men totally unable to help. The fine dainty ladies, every one of them down to the last lace handkerchief, had forged to the front and secured the ringside seats first. We poor men were pushed to the rear. Never had the slightest chance. Of course, the ladies all set up a sympathetic roar. Perry, that little blighter of Dimmity's, yapped and snarled with the best of them. Then Clare, unable to contain herself any longer, swooned—unerringly on top of Perry. Admittedly, the wisest thing she has ever done. Dimmity, however, took exception, thinking Poor Pwecious had cut his stick. Becoming hysterical, she flung herself into her dear papa's arms.

"Well, old Childers, none too steady at any time and positively rickety after a night of drink, was not up to Dimmity's weight. Over they went, on top of Clare—

102

appropriate retribution, I would say. I'd have laid a monkey then that Perry had stuck his spoon in the wall for good, but the little beast . . . pluck to the backbone, he proved the first to crawl out from the pile. He shook himself once and then, like the fine male that he is, toddled to Uncle's rescue and clamped his canine's into Blanche. The intrepid critter hung on bravely until she boxed his ears for his trouble. I've never seen a poodle pirouette like that before!"

Megan laughed till the tears sparkled in her eyes. "Oh, how I wish I could have been there," she moaned, holding her sides. "Wed Blanche, Justin. Please do. She deserves something for her courageous performance."

"And I should be the prize?" Justin asked, astonished.

"Well, you did say you were the catch of the season."

"I can see the headline in the *Gazette,* now— 'Argyle Bartered Off By Upstairs Maid. Sold To Woman Bruiser As Catch Of The Season. No, my dear, I don't hold myself that cheap. Can you see the life I would lead shackled to LaBlanche? If I were late in the least, she'd box my ears like a grubby schoolboy's."

"I still hold she is the best of the lot. No die-away miss there." Megan still remembered Malissa's comments.

"You would champion her, termagant." Justin thought the two ladies similar in their intrepid manner, but Blanche did not have Megan's leavening humor or dignity—Meg with dignity? Ha! "Remember, my fine miss, if I marry her, I will make sure you suffer. I'll make you her personal maid."

Megan refrained from comment. At times like these her deception sent daggers of guilt shooting throughout her body. She smiled weakly and said, "Blanche is not the only one among your possible intendeds with a

103

strong arm."

"Oh, and who else?"

"You'd never guess, but the sensitive Clare can fling an exceptional hairbrush."

"Pray do tell."

"I was walking past her rooms when I heard the angriest words. The door flew open and Marie, Clare's maid, came spewing out. To my incomprehension, she flung herself to one side of the wall. A hairbrush followed directly, at no mean speed. Marie picked it up after it had boomeranged off the wall and said, with calm composure, 'I dodge the brush well, non?'"

"Well, that settles it. Clare is off my list," Justin said firmly. "I refuse to marry a hairbrush thrower—God only knows what else she might throw. Brummel may cavail at marrying a woman who eats cabbage, but I draw the mark at the one who throws brushes."

"But Justin, other than this penchant for pegging an occasional hairbrush, Clare is truly a talented young lady. I've heard her play the pianoforte beautifully and her watercolours are exquisite."

"But she is hypercritically sensitive, Meg," Justin insisted. Clare apparently was tempermental and that would never do. He did not mind a woman of spirit—look how he tolerated Meggy's fits and starts—but Clare's temperament stemmed from self-consequence only. She put on airs for herself and no one else.

"Well, that leaves Dimmity to be your lady. She really is a lovely child, Justin—so comfortable."

Justin looked at Meggy's sincere blue eyes and wondered what slight differences in colour could affect. Dimmity's were vapid, with something missing. They would never be able to hold fire or intelligence like Megan's did.

Now if Justin had analyzed his thoughts, he might have learned something very surprising. Yet the most intelligent of people are also the ones who refuse to listen to their feelings or lend them the least consideration. Justin looked easily at his helpful, unusual maid and said, "Yes, Meg, she would be acceptable, but combine her with Perry and I could never survive."

"Ignore Perry. You are marrying the woman, not the dog. Dimmity is very fetching and biddable. I've heard said her lisp is all the crack in town—just imagine the sweet nothings she could whisper in your ear."

"While Perry snapped and growled in the other? No thank you, Meggy. The succession can be hanged before I take that dreadful step. The sad fact is, Perry's conversation might prove more intelligent than Dim--mity's."

Ignoring this palpable hit, Megan retorted, "Honestly, Justin, you ask too much of women. You may construct your cynical front, but you are at fault. You are looking for a goddess."

"A goddess? I wonder if Mother would think her good enough for me? We'd definitely have to check her bloodline, must be English, you know, none of these foreign Greek ladies that are no better than they ought to be."

"Which makes you no different than anyone else," Megan persisted. "You wish to marry for love, for that is the only way you will ever be able to accept a woman totally. There are only human goddesses when it's in the eyes of love."

"Meggy, you are such a romantic. But I refuse to pull caps with you today. You must admit we did not find the crème de la crème here."

'But they're the top of the ton," Megan said—and then had to admit that they were not the most exciting of ladies.

"There must be an unexceptional heiress somewhere I can marry," Justin mused. "What do you say I send this house party packing and look for new game?"

"Justin, surely you cannot be so cruel! And I'm sure you wouldn't wish to send Malissa away," Megan added, unable to stop herself.

"Oh, wouldn't I?" Justin asked without expression.

"Perhaps," Megan replied, not knowing what possessed her, "you should call off the hunt and settle on Malissa. There is no doubt that she cares for you and you two seem to deal . . . famously together."

Justin gazed at her a moment. "Take Malissa to wife?" When he saw that Megan was dead earnest, he shook his head.

"She truly cares for you . . ." Megan turned her head away.

"Meggy, Meggy, what a child you are. You do not even understand your own kind, let alone we fickle men. Which fairyland did you wander from? God forbid, who let you loose on the world?"

"Oh, my revolutionary grandf—ah, fate!" Meggy laughed quickly.

"Well, they always said fate was unkind," Justin said suddenly. "No, the guests must go, all of them. I have decided." He didn't want to think of Megan's fate—or his own, for that matter.

"But Justin," Megan protested, "they intend to stay another week. You will cut up all their hopes!"

"Exactly." The Earl rose and sauntered from the barn. "Besides, I must see an end to your exile and Mother's travails. She's in high fidgets over her special rose—or violet, no matter—and she doesn't know how to go on. I will tell you something, if you do not become too puffed up in your own conceit. You are so important that Mother is scouring the house for that 'nice, petit point maid.' You must have proven worthy, for she even remembers that your name starts with 'm.' Though she cannot come to the right one—she's called

106

you Melisande, Megan, Margaret, Melinda, and many other fine names, but she has not yet hit on Meggy."

Megan gasped, but Justin had delivered this unwitting Parthian shot and departed. Willing her pulse to calm, she thought that the fates must have a very ill humor indeed. She prayed that she might survive her masquerade. Then looking down at her pained ankle, she uttered an unladylike curse.

Chapter Seven

More Sword, More Suprises

Within two days, the Earl had cleared Argyle Court of its guests, the mothers very miffed, the daughters sunk in fits of blue depression. Even Malissa was sent packing. She left regally, but underneath, fear grasped her heart. She wanted Justin, not just as a lover, but as her next husband. He was a prize she did not intend to lose.

Yet she was losing him. She could not discover what had cooled his ardor. Certainly this gaggle of silly geese did not attract him—what did? He had not come to her once, though he merely said it was improper to do so in his mother's house.

He said he would return to town soon. She had another chance. She could not fail when next she saw him.

As Justin watched the last overloaded carriage creak away, he closed the door with a heartfelt sigh. He looked around and realized that he had not seen Edward for days. He was as difficult to find as Meg. A quick, unworthy suspicion took hold of him only to be laughed away. Meggy and Edward at a rendezvous could only be comical.

He found himself sauntering back to the kitchen to see Mrs. Bodkins, as he had so often done as a youth. She was there, busily directing Cook. "Hallo, Mrs. Bodkins, light of my life, how are you today?"

Mrs. Bodkins beamed upon him. "Go on with ye, Master Justin, such a flatterer. What can I do for ye?"

"I'm looking for that young scamp I call brother." Justin reached for a turnover cooling on the sheet. The Corinthian of London was promptly snapped on the wrist with Mrs. Bodkins' long spoon. Justin remembered why he loved Argyle Court.

"I'm not sure where he is, Master Justin," Mrs. Bodkins said evasively.

"Come, Body, you know where everyone is."

'Aye, that I do," she agreed, no proof against his pet name for her. "I think he is out fencing—ah, practicing fencing, that is."

Justin started out the door, then stopped to inquire as an afterthought, "By the by, Body, where is that maid, Meggy?"

Mrs. Bodkins shifted uneasily. "I think she is out checking on Mrs. Timeble—she's about due and Meggy wanted to make sure she was well."

"You sent Meggy?" Sternness crept into Justin's voice. "That is a job for a doctor or midwife, not a young girl."

"But she be frightful good at doctoring, my Lord." Cook piped up. "She's helped my rheumatism no end. That girl's got a smooth and gentle touch."

"Aye, Master Justin, she's got what they call the healing touch," Mrs. Bodkins agreed. "It comes natural. Dr. James has been visiting his sick aunt, so Meggy's been a help. The midwife will be there for Mrs. Timble," she added, as Justin frowned.

"Well, I'm going to see Edward," Justin said, and left. Cook and Mrs. Bodkins looked at each other with worried eyes. Cook crossed herself.

As Justin opened the door to the practice room, he was surprised to hear Edward swearing in a low growl. Was he talking to himself? "Blasted, you play the innocent, and just when I think I've got you, you slip away!"

Justin was astounded to hear Meggy's taunting laughter. "Come, Edward, try again. I certainly enjoy your tactics, so rough and furious."

"I will have you at my mercy yet, Meggy my dear, begging for release."

"Come on then," she chuckled. "Do not just play with me."

"What the devil?" Justin asked himself.

"My foil is not unsheathed for nothing," Edward said. "I have a few new moves that should please you. And I've been strengthening my thrust!"

"What the devil!" the Earl repeated in shock. He swung the door open.

What he saw, he hardly expected. At first he thought Edward fought another man, for Meggy was nowhere to be seen. Then the thunderous realization struck Justin. Edward's opponent was no gentleman, but his erstwhile maid!

He stood transfixed as Edward gave an outraged howl and lunged at Meggy. Their foils rang as she parried his blow.

With surprise, Justin noted considerable skill on both sides. Edward was fast, yet Meggy was more fluid and sure, parrying his blows, then riposting swiftly. Her feints and disengages were subtle and smooth. Where had she learned her tactics?

Edward finally pulled back to wipe the sweat from his eyes. Meggy laughed breathlessly, her white shirt clinging to her, wet with perspiration. Justin noted rather closely that she was breathing heavily.

He perused her trim, full figure, now in baggy britches, while her tawny hair was pulled back loosely in a queue. Shock coursed through him—whether it was at her form of dress or his own reaction to it, he could not determine. To see a woman only in dresses and then see her garbed in such a different manner was like seeing her unclad for the first time. He pushed such thoughts from his mind when he heard Edward's boyish laugh again.

"I wouldn't laugh too loudly Edward, she held you at bay rather effectively." Justin decided to attack his brother first; the two miscreants turned glowing, unabashed faces toward him.

"Justin, what are you doing here, old man? So you've discovered our hideaway." Justin flinched at Edward's words. "You're right, this woman is a witch. She acts as if she knows nothing about nothing and suddenly she trounces me with a clever feint. She must have spent all night practicing, just to put me in the shade. She's a viper!"

Megan followed Edward's lead in making light of it, though she could see that Justin was none too pleased. "Unjust Edward, I don't slander you merely because you score a hit or two, which is often enough."

Listening to the two joking fencers, Justin relaxed. Sometimes he wondered that he hadn't done enough with Edward; once or twice he had glimpsed the loneliness in him. Evidently Meggy had also. "I'm glad you don't always best him. I would fear for the overweening growth of your pride."

"So true, Brother, the chit is too insolent by far," Edward goodheartedly agreed. Walking over to Justin, he proffered his blade. "Try your hand at it Justin, but watch it. She's slippery as an eel."

111

Justin hesitated, but then accepted the foil. Walking over, he slid out of his jacket and Hessians. Turning, he took his stance opposite Megan.

Blue eyes smiled seriously into grey; Edward, surprised, felt the calm challenge that sprang up between the two. His laughing brother and joking maid had changed of a sudden, and both wore an odd, quiet smile.

"En garde," Justin commanded. Saluting, both adopted the en garde position.

For Edward, it was as if he watched a strange minuet. Their forms bent and flowed, graceful and strong. He watched as they parried and thrust, completely in tune with each other; entranced, he hardly realized the rapidly increasing pace and the dangerous flash of the foils. Caught in their intensity, he started when Justin pulled back from his final lunge so that the blade only grazed Megan's shoulder as it swung upward.

Wrenched from his trance, Edward's eyes flew to the tip of Justin's foil. He groaned; there was no button. He and Meggy had been practicing for quite a while—he should have checked the blade before surrendering it to Justin.

Justin stood in tense consternation, eyes riveted upon Megan, who had gasped before gaining control. Avoiding his gaze, she calmly set the foil down. There was a burning sensation, but instinct told her the wound was negligible. The frozen worry in Justin's eyes was not.

"It is nought but a scratch, Justin," Megan assured him quietly. "Edward, could you please bring a handkerchief?"

Justin's eyes fell to the redness seeping slowly across her shirt. He broke from his stance and strode over. "Will he never lose that panther grace?" Megan sighed

TAKE ADVANTAGE OF THIS SPECIAL OFFER, AVAILABLE *ONLY* TO ZEBRA REGENCY ROMANCE READERS.

You are a reader who enjoys the very special kind of love story that can only be found in Zebra Regency Romances. You adore the fashionable English settings, the sparkling wit, the captivating intrigue, and the heart-stirring romance that are the hallmarks of each Zebra Regency Romance novel.

Now, you can have these delightful novels delivered right to your door each month and never have to worry about missing a new book. Zebra has made arrangements through its Home Subscription Service for you to preview the three latest Zebra Regency Romances as soon as they are published.

3 **FREE** REGENCIES TO GET STARTED!

To get your subscription started, we will send your first 3 books ABSOLUTELY FREE, as our introductory gift to you. NO OBLIGATION. We're sure that you will enjoy these books so much that you will want to read more of the very best romantic fiction published today.

SUBSCRIBERS SAVE EACH MONTH

Zebra Regency Home Subscribers will save money each month as they enjoy their latest Regencies. As a subscriber you will receive the 3 newest titles to preview FREE for ten days. Each shipment will be at least a $11.97 value (publisher's price). But home subscribers will be billed only $9.90 for all three books. You'll save over $2.00 each month. Of course, if you're not satisfied with any book, just return it for full credit.

FREE HOME DELIVERY

Zebra Home Subscribers get free home delivery. There are never any postage, shipping or handling charges. No hidden charges. What's more, there is no minimum number to buy and you can cancel your subscription at any time. No obligation and no questions asked.

to herself. It made a girl nervous.

"Let me see the wound."

"No, Justin. It is but a scratch, certainly not a wound." Megan made her denial as calm as possible.

"Then let me see it." Frowning, he reached toward her. She backed away evasively.

"You are not a doctor; it is fine," she said sharply.

"There you are out, Meg," Edward said, striving to lighten the charged atmosphere; Justin and Megan had pugnaciously squared off by this time. "He is a very good doctor—though I hear his bedside manner is even better."

"Heed the young man. Let me see it, Meggy." Justin flashed her a quick, warm smile. "I won't be satisfied if you don't."

"Then you will remain unsatisfied."

Edward went to her and handed her the handkerchief. "Meg, don't be such a clunch." His eyes lit with a swift gleam. "Why don't you ask Justin to show you his old wound in exchange for you showing him your new one. It's only fair."

Megan glanced at Justin with interest. His grey eyes gleamed wickedly down at her. "I'll accept. Would you like to see it, Meggy?"

"First I'd like to know how you received it. Could it have come from being overbearing?"

"No, no, Meg. It was strictly a matter of honor," Edward choked out. Megan's sweetly delivered slur had caught him off guard.

"Well, I am glad for that. However, I do not desire to view this—ah—wound of honor. I have a feeling it would be decidedly improper. Now, if you two gentlemen will excuse me, I must take this paltry scratch off and attend it."

"Meggy, blast it, let me see it!" Justin demanded, suddenly furious.

"No!"

"You are my servant. Let me see it!" He pulled her hand and then the handkerchief away from her shoulder. Megan froze at this. With a frown, he slid the shirt off her shoulder to inspect the wound. A simple process, since Jed's shirts were not tailor-made. "Do you never wear clothes that fit?"

"Gads, Meggy, you possess a shoulder," Edward expounded in feigned astonishment. "The way your hackles raised, I thought you must have a hunchback or two hidden away there. 'Tis a fair shoulder, I'd say—wouldn't you, Justin?"

Justin merely grunted. As he reached to touch her, Megan backed away hastily. She had learned that for some inexplicable reason, Justin's touch unsettled her. If she started to shake, he was sure to think her ill.

Slapping his hand away, she jerked her shirt into place, glaring at the two. "I'm perfectly fine!" Turning, she stalked out grandly.

Edward clapped Justin on the back consolingly. "She may be your servant, Justin, and she may be a damn fine fencer, but, alas, she is also all woman—totally and irrevocably unpredictable. Go light on her."

Ignoring Edward, Justin swore savagely and flung out after Megan. He followed her with long, angry strides, pulling her roughly to a stop when he caught her.

"Hell and confound it, Meggy, must you countermand every order—nay, request!—that I give you? You insubordinate, hot-at-hand, little idiot, I ought to horsewhip you and have done with your tantrums!"

"Go right ahead! Are you going to ask to see the lashings afterward?"

"What are you insinuating?" Justin demanded. His eyebrows soared as he looked down his patrician nose. "I have no need to importune innocent females. I am

114

not a ravisher of virgins!" He proclaimed it in a voice the whole countryside could hear.

"For that I am forever thankful, my Lord, otherwise this employment would be far too loathsome to me!"

Justin shook her in incredulous fury. No woman had ever said that to him before. For too long, women had been happy to have his tall, rangy body beside them in polite conversation—or otherwise. "Meggy, I could strangle you."

"Just don't ravish me," Meggy retorted. Her anger faded into embarrassment as she realized it was she who had expressed the first base thoughts.

She looked down quickly, trying to hide her rising flush. Stunned, Justin studied her bent, tawny head. He remembered her injury. He had actually shaken her. He wished urgently that he could hold her and stop her trembling (a remedy Megan could have told him was doomed to fail). What was the matter with him? "Dammit, woman—I'm sorry. I suppose I was overly concerned. I did not think you to be so missish." Slowly he released her arms, but his words cut Megan to the quick.

"I am not missish. It's just that I am still not accustomed to orders. I . . . I was left very much on my own and pretty much did what I wanted when I grew up. I guess I am not a very good servant," she concluded self-consciously.

"That you are not." Justin's smile softened the edges of his statement. "Now go and tend to that wound—I fear I have hindered what I sought to help. Please keep me informed. I do not wish it to scar."

"It will not," Megan said, brightening. "Oh Justin, can we continue to fence? You have skills I would dearly love to learn . . . so would Edward," she added belatedly.

"Yes, Meggy. Now please go tend to that wound

before you bleed to death out of sheer contrariness."

"Oh, I couldn't do that," Megan assured him impishly. "It's already stopped bleeding. It was only a scratch."

Justin smiled in exasperation as he watched Megan striding off in her man's clothes. The outfit wasn't all that bad once one grew accustomed to it.

A frown marred Justin's brow as he studied the missive in his hand. It represented the end of an ideal two weeks, uniquely filled with sports and leisure. His department had recalled him to London. He bent and wrote a terse reply, and handed it to the quiet, nondescript man awaiting it. Justin saw him out, then turned on his heel to hunt out Mrs. Bodkins and inquire the whereabouts of Edward and Meggy.

"The children be out fishing," Mrs. Bodkins replied without thought.

"Ah, well, I believe I will join them."

As Justin left, Mrs. Bodkins considered what she had said. For the past two weeks all three, Meggy, Justin, and Edward, had acted very much like overgrown children. Meggy would hurry through her chores and when Justin's estate business was finished, the three would venture forth for fencing, riding, and shooting.

A pretty state of affairs it was, Mrs. Bodkins clucked to herself, with her Ladyship chasing about like a hoyden. No good would come of it, as she was sure Mr. Tothwell would say, if that worthy were advised of these matters. Yet she could not bring herself to bear tales, especially when both her dear boys enjoyed themselves so heartily. Master Justin had eased into the warm-hearted lad of his youth, rather than the reserved, austere man he had become. As for Master Edward, well, he basked in his brother's companionship. No, she could not bring herself to cry rope on her Ladyship; she could only pray that no harm would fall that impetuous, madcap lady.

Justin, in heavy thought, proceeded across the field and through the cove to the stream. He halted on the rise, well-hidden in the trees, and studied the diverting picture of Megan and Edward applying themselves to the serious business of fishing.

Remains of a picnic lay scattered amongst poles and lines. Two relaxed figures lay close to the water, their poles barely secured in lazy grasps. Shoes, apparently kicked off without care, lay beside the fervent fishermen.

Megan spoke, looking disparagingly at the bucket next to her. "Edward, your vaunted luck that you so rashly puffed off has gone fishing elsewhere today."

"Burn it! I can't understand it," Edward complained in hurt tones. "We've not had an infernal nibble all morning."

"Perhaps you did all the eating for them," Megan suggested, eyeing the last remnants of the food.

"Well, I like that! I had to fight my way for every minute crumb I could capture!"

"Fie, Edward, fair is fair! The last sandwich was mine."

"Devil take it, it ain't decent the way you tuck in. Ain't never seen such a trencherwoman."

"I have spent many sleepless nights over my sad want of delicacy—alack that I cannot eat like a bird. I confess I am a blight to my gender!" Megan moaned.

"Don't roast me, old girl. You'll gain no sympathy from me." Edward was undeceived by Megan's lachrymose tone. "Any more of that from you and I'll throw you in a dungeon and feed you bread and water!"

"You have a dungeon here at Argyle?" Megan said excitedly.

"No, sad to say. Only wishing I had one. Shames me to say it, but the family ain't that romantical. If we had one, would have walled it in ages ago, or made a dashed wine cellar out of it, what?"

"Well, what a bubble!" exclaimed Megan in disappointment.

Suddenly Edward's pole bent into the water. Edward exclaimed and jumped up.

"Yoicks, to hounds men, to hounds! I've got one, strap me if it ain't a giant!" He pulled in a frenzy, executing such footwork that even those proud dames of Almacks would have approved.

Megan shrieked with a total lack of decorum and scrambled out of Edward's range. "Have a care!" But he'd already kicked her shoes into the water. "There went my shoes."

Edward never heard her, so intent was he in landing his whale. But, alas, to every blind fanaticism there is generally a nemesis. Caesar had his Brutus, Edward had his bucket, the very one that was to hold the demonic fish he battled so frantically. He crashed into it, sending his pole flying. The pole made a steady bee-line into the stream and sunk.

Off-balanced, Edward flapped his arms wildly, resembling nothing more than an ungainly pelican desperate to take flight. He did not fly, however, and the resounding splash mercifully drowned his next word.

Edward surfaced spitting water, a grim Poseidon.

"Oh no Edward," Megan gurgled, collapsing on the ground in laughter. "I'm dreadfully sorry, I know I shouldn't laugh—but you look so funny!"

118

Finally rising, she hopped to the water's edge and offered her hand to the approaching Edward. He took it. "Meggy, I don't mind telling you that it ain't civil, it ain't civil at all to laugh at others' misfortunes." He pulled her into the stream with him. "For, alas, that same misfortune might befall yourself."

Justin watching, finally gave forth a shout of laughter. He sauntered from his secluded spot, applauding handsomely. "Bravo, bravo! Let that be a laudable lesson to you, Meg."

Indignant, Megan prepared to deliver a stinging retort, then she caught Edward's gleaming eye. He winked at her and nodded.

Justin, his native intelligence too far submerged in the enjoyment of the moment, only stood laughing as the sodden couple advanced from the water. The next instant, he was grasped on both sides and pulled into the stream.

He surfaced and gaped at them incredulously. For one baited moment, each watched the other furtively. Simultaneously, they all broke into laughter.

"In truth, it is rude to laugh at another's misfortune," Megan sputtered.

"Surely you agree, Justin," Edward chuckled. "I heard you say it with my own ears."

"Ah, so did I, curse my unruly tongue. Now I wonder what horrible punishment I should meet out to you two worrisome scamps," he mused, dashing water from his eyes. "Odd, my faculties fail me. I can't seem to generate proper thoughts in this drenched state."

"Ha! I would gladly face the rack for the pleasure of seeing your expression when you surfaced," Edward exclaimed. "Gads, what a lark." He splashed to shore, Justin following.

Only Megan remained, and this through no desire of her own, for upon her first step, her skirts wrapped

119

about her like a lovelorn octopus. She fell back, got up, and fell back again with a splash.

Justin turned around at this, and quickly assessed her difficulties. All he said was, "Come, Meggy, don't dawdle." He waded back in and offered her his hand. "We'll need to get out of these clothes if we aren't to fall victim to an inflammation of the lungs."

Once tugged to shore, Megan was grateful to stand on dry land. her hair hung in sodden clumps and her wet dress clung to her in the most revealing fashion. Justin cast her a cursory glance, then turned abruptly away. Edward, however, cleared the water from his eyes and stared at her. "We'd best hie ourselves to the house. Might not be aware of this, old girl, but those clothes ain't decent anymore. Better get out of them—wouldn't want to appear improper."

"I'd be a far sight more improper without them," Megan pointed out reasonably.

"Come! I don't intend to stand about while you two imps debate," Justin grinned. "Let's go make a decent woman out of Meggy—after all, you were the cause of her fall, Edward."

"Here, now! Don't want to add to my reputation!" retorted Edward.

Edward and Justin met no impediment to making good their decision to leave, their Hessians sloshing in happy union. Poor Megan lacked even the shoes to slosh in. Gamely, she teetered and skipped across the forest floor, stubbing her toe on a limb that must have lain in wait for one such as she. She howled and bent to nurse her injured foot. Justin turned once again. "Meggy, bustle about, we'll still be here at nightfall at this pace."

"I am walking as fast as I can, but it is no simple matter. However did the savages go on without shoes?" Meggy was amazed at the new view of things she possessed. For all her voluptuous curves, she resembled nothing more than a child in her bedraggled and barefoot state. "I have already had two loathsome stickers attach themselves to me. What shocking toadies!"

"Here! Here! The Lady needs rescuing from such importunities! A call for chivalry!" Edward declaimed with a thrilled voice. "Justin, be a good fellow and carry Meg."

"What, is this chivalry by proxy?"

"Well, must own it, old man, you possess more of the brawn than I. Wouldn't do for me to drop Meg, that couldn't help her one whit. In fact, could cause her great injury and me great pain!"

Megan laughed. "Oh, how enchanting to be the object of such gallantry! But let us hear no more on this head. I will walk myself to the house. I do not care to be bartered off between you two eager gallants."

"Forsooth, fair maiden!" Justin clasped her hand and smiled down into her eyes. "Do not deny me." With a swift movement, he swung her into his arms. Before she had a chance to rally and struggle, he had secured her.

"Justin, put me down, I am far too heavy!" demanded a flustered Megan.

In truth, Justin found Megan no light weight, yet she was a comfortable armful. He judged that he could carry her with no difficulty. "No, Meg, I assure you I can manage. Now stop wiggling and put your arms around me, or I will put you down and none too lightly."

Hearing the iron determination behind his banter, Megan could not doubt it. Unless she intended to brangle all the way back, she would have to submit. She slid her arms hesitantly around Justin's neck. He made a quick movement as if to drop her and she

121

hugged him tightly. "Ah, decidedly better."

"Well, I'm glad that's settled." Edward nodded cheerily. "Strap me if I've ever met a more fractious female than you, Meg."

Megan's contrariness was in abeyance at the moment. Being carried by Justin was proving another of the unsettling experiences that Megan had suffered since her arrival at Argyle.

Her wet clothes seemed nonexistent, so little shielding did they provide. They felt like the proverbial second skin; dry, she had felt protected, but now wet, she felt terribly vulnerable. Body heat steamed through the damp clothes, moulding her to Justin in a disquieting, but not unpleasant state.

Megan's pulse quickened of its own accord while her heart thumped crazily. Surely Justin couldn't help but notice, with her heart so close to his chest. Megan looked down, unable to say a word. Strangely enough, Justin didn't, either.

Edward followed behind the two stiff, silent people, bewildered. Suddenly, his eyes widened with disbelief. He, too, looked down, whistling tunelessly in abstraction.

A very subdued trio made its way to the back kitchen entrance. Edward opened the door to let Justin and his armful enter. Mrs. Bodkins turned from the fire in surprise. "Why, what do we have here, Master Justin? Is it a mermaid ye've caught, lad?"

"I don't believe so, Mrs. Bodkins. Her—ah, dorsal fin seems quite different," Justin joked, giving that particular area a small pat.

Megan surfaced from her trance at this. "You can put me down, my Lord."

"Aye, that ye'd better, Master Justin," Mrs. Bodkins agreed sharply. "The lass might think ye have no manners."

122

"I'm sorry, Mrs. Bodkins," Justin apologized in mock contrition. "I fear they were drowned in the stream, along with Meggy's shoes."

"Aye, now I ken. What happened? Did ye decide to go swimming?" Mrs. Bodkins was familiar with accidents and play.

"How perceptive. That we did, Mrs. Bodkins," Edward offered. "It was all Meggy's idea. She can swim like a fish."

"And she can drink like one, too," Justin murmured into Megan's ear as he set her down. A responding "hush" hissed through her teeth.

"Oh, Mrs. Bodkins, do you have a mushroom?" A voice drifted in from the entryway, then Lady Augusta arrived to claim it. "Meggy highly recommended that I study the things I petit point, which, now that I think of it, makes uncommonly good sense. It seems to make a difference . . . oh." Lady Augusta discovered her dripping offspring and maid. "Hello, dears. Justin, sweetheart, do you know that you are quite wet?"

"Yes, Mother, I had noticed."

"Why are you wet?"

"Well, Mother—"

Edward interrupted. "We went fishing, Mother."

"Oh? Where are the fish? Not that I wish to see them, they do smell so. And they just stare balefully until one is overcome with guilt, even if one didn't have a hand in catching them."

"They are—in the pond," Edward said.

"That would explain it." Lady Augusta's knowing nod threw the others into confusion. "Perhaps you felt guilty too?"

"Ah, yes," Edward agreed. "We returned them to the stream . . . personally."

"So I see. Well, I'm glad Charles was never wet when he returned from fishing. You must have a change in

123

the sport. You men are always creating sports that have little purpose, like those dreadful fisticuffs. Though why you should have taken Megan along is beyond me. You are asking too much from the girl. Remember, sons, one should always be understanding of one's servants."

"Yes, Mother." Justin quickly stemmed the airy flow of chatter. "Now, Mother, I must inform you that I must return to London on the morrow. I must be gone a fortnight or so."

"Ah, Justin!" Edward felt quite disappointed. "Must you leave? We were having such a jolly good time!" Megan, though she would sooner be nibbled to death by a duck than admit it, wanted to wail the same thing. She quickly hid her disappointment, for Justin was studying her face as closely as his family's.

"Sorry, Edward. This is on business."

"Certainly, business with a certain brunette." A needle of hurt threaded his voice. Justin clapped him on the shoulder.

"No, halfling, it isn't. This is a matter of some importance."

"Oh, dear, Justin, must you?" his mother queried. "Well, if you must, you must. You know, I wish you did not, but I understand." Megan was often amazed at the understanding Lady Augusta had for her men.

Justin gave his mother a singularly tender smile and went to kiss her on the forehead. "Thank you, mother dearest. I shan't be longer than I have to. Come, Edward, I challenge you to a game of chess."

Justin looked back once at Megan, and then the family left the kitchen. Megan fumed. Maid she might be, but Justin could have said goodbye. He could have said goodbye!

Chapter Eight

Gallant Night

Megan rolled over to swat her pillow viciously, sighing. It had been almost two weeks (one week and four days, to be exact) since Justin left. Edward had promptly deserted to visit friends and Argyle Court had sunk into the doldrums. It amazed Megan that she had ever wished for an unpopulated, Earl-free establishment. An Egyptian tomb would rank as a squeeze compared to Argyle Court at present.

As she tossed for the sixtieth time she heard a distant clatter. Ceasing her revolutions and sitting up on her elbow, she stared wide-eyed into the darkness. There it was again, only fainter.

Temptation gnawed at Megan, who was already in a restive state of mind. Finally something to do—investigating the noise would be a much more enjoyable pastime than shredding her feather pillow. Cracking open her room's door, she quietly stepped into the hall.

Candle in hand, Megan moved stealthily toward the sound she thought she had heard in the front foyer.

Moonlight illuminated the hall, washing the marble floors to ghostly white, shaping the shadows into phantoms. Holding her candle high, she spied upon the floor a silver dish that had obviously clattered off the new curio table Crispins had proudly placed in the foyer a week before. Now how had it fallen off?

Suddenly, an iron hand came from behind and covered her mouth, relentlessly pulling her to a struggling halt against a tall, hard body. Megan tugged and flailed to no avail. She succeeded only in dropping her candle. Almost choking in exasperation, she kicked at the flame, extinguishing it.

Megan might have saved the house from fire, but now the room was ink black. Wonderful! Megan thought as she struggled, her heart a pounding pianissimo.

Was her captor made of stone? She had to be the only woman ever attacked by a walking statue. Stopping her ineffectual railing, she settled for the one small satisfaction available. Angrily, she sunk her teeth into the hand that so rudely muzzled her mouth.

Her neck cracked as her head was roughly jerked backward. Then a warm breath tickled her ear. "Please, Meggy, that is my hand, not a piece of meat." The offending hand was slowly removed from between her teeth.

"Justin?"

"At your service, my dear."

His encircling arms now loose, Megan twisted around and peered at him. "My God, you look awful!"

"You overwhelm me with such compliments," Justin said with a tired smile. Dark shadows rimmed his eyes and bruises hollowed out his face. A cut scratched across his forehead.

Justin slowly sagged within Megan's arms. Convulsively, she grasped him closer. She felt a warm

126

stickiness. "My God, you are hurt. There is blood!"

"Yes. Unfortunately, it is mine."

"Are you hurt badly?"

"'Tis nothing but a scratch," Justin mimicked in a prim voice.

"Be quiet! And hold onto me.

"With pleasure," he breathed.

Megan tottered, but regained her balance. "Please don't let us fall down this time," she prayed as, more and more, Justin leaned on her. "Thank heaven I'm not the petite damsel." She held him all the closer.

Counting each step as a victory, Megan pushed Justin across the foyer, dreaming of getting him safely to his room. Finally, she reached the stairs, only to look up in dawning horror. She groaned; Justin raised his head and joined her. "Damn, we'll never make it, Meg. You've got to help me. I don't want anyone to know I'm here."

Megan bit her tongue and did not say a word—not even to ask the reasonable question of whether he still possessed sanity. Panting from her exertions, she numbly turned Justin's six-foot frame away from the stairs and toward her room. Her nerves stretched as Justin remained silent, only his heavy breathing accompanied her own gasps. "Stay with me, Justin. Stay with me!"

"I have no intention of running," Justin murmured after a moment. "And if you are very good, I promise not to faint."

Megan could not resist a chuckle as she propped Justin against the wall and opened her bedroom door. "How generous of you, monsieur." She knew what it cost him to admit that. Wrapping her arms around him once again, she assisted him to her bed, sat him down, and eased him back slowly.

"Is this your room?" Justin suddenly focused and

127

looked around.

"Yes."

"I hope your intentions are honorable, Meggy." Justin leaned back on the pillow, grimacing.

"Will you stop joking?" Megan snapped. She was unnerved by Justin's pallor and the crimson staining his shirt, hopelessly mesmerized by it. "Justin, I have to get Dr. James. I'll be right back."

"No," Justin groaned out through clenched teeth

"I am going to get a doctor!"

"No, Meggy, I forbid it. No one must know that I am here."

"You are the stubbornest man," Megan exclaimed. "What am I to do with your corpse should you choose to die? Hide it under the bed so no one knows you are here?"

"How gruesome, my dear. It is not as bad as that. Please—Meggy, they say you are a good doctor. Help me." Justin's grey eyes pierced hers, gently compelling her.

Megan shook her head, eyes snapping. He reached his good hand out and stooped to a pleading smile. The devil fly away with the man! "All right."

She stalked out to return shortly with warm water, bandages, becillum powder, and a bottle of brandy. Setting the items none too gently on the nightstand, she handed Justin the bottle of brandy. "Have a few sips of this, but no more." She refused to look at him.

Perching gingerly on the edge of the bed, Megan reached over and loosened Justin's cravat, then undid his shirt, though the buttons refused to let go. Always cool and efficient with other patients, her fingers shook uncontrollably with this one.

Justin froze, the bottle arrested in midair, as Megan's unsteady fingers lightly pushed back his shirt. She hesitated briefly at the sight of his smooth chest,

128

lightly furred with hair, but fiercely she turned her attention to the wound etched across his right side. It was deep, but not dangerous, thank God.

Silently she took the bottle from Justin, got up, and set it on the bureau. She drew a deep breath, came back, and undid his cuffs, easing him out of his shirt. A tension grew; neither felt comfortable with these domestic chores. But with as much professionalism as possible, Megan washed the wound, powdered it, and bandaged it.

Justin resisted watching her hands as they touched and tended his side. His eyes never strayed from Megan's concerned face, a deep and guarded look descending upon his own. Yes, he thought, Mrs. B. was right. Megan did have the healing touch. Her fingers were gentle and light, but burned with a concern and calm, almost cauterizing the wound. He swiftly closed his eyes as Megan turned to wash and bandage his face.

"Concentrate, stupid!" Megan commanded herself as she cleaned the scratch on his cheek. Yet her eyes searched his every feature, gleefully drinking them in in a leisurely and undetected perusal. Sable lashes lay against strong cheekbones, the firm, sensual lips in sculptured repose below.

Megan called herself back to task in disgust, and, grabbing the bandages and pan, whisked them over to the bureau. Keeping her back to Justin, she feigned busyness, attempting to calm her nerves.

Now that he'd been attended to, Justin felt his strength seeping back, exhaustion now being his major wound. He studied the small, neat room: the bed, a side table, and the bureau were the sole furniture. There would be no place for Meggy to sleep if one ruled out the bed, or the floor. He definitely ruled out the floor. He'd bet a monkey that Meggy would rule out the bed.

Closing his eyes in feigned rest, he pondered a

129

moment. Opening them, he cast a speculative glance at Meg, who was still straightening and restraightening the supplies. A slow, mischievous smile curled his lips. He was not the resourceful Earl of Argyle for nothing.

Slouching down, he flung one concealing arm over his eyes and let out a deathly moan. Megan jumped and spun around.

"Justin, are you all right?" She rushed over and bent down to him solicitously. He groaned again, weakly. She smoothed his hair out of his eyes and laid her hand upon his forehead.

This time, he mumbled—indistinguishable, frenzied words. She was forced to bend closer to hear them.

"Justin, where is it hurting you?" Megan was frightened—his forehead felt confusingly cool. Lord, she had hoped to avoid the fever. "Justin, can you hear me?"

"Mother, is that you?" Justin groped out blindly and pulled Megan breath-snatchingly close.

Megan now found herself in the awkward position of being clutched to a delirious man's chest. "Justin, hush . . ." She tried to right herself. "I'm not your mother, I'm your maid, remember?"

"Oh Mother, you're here." Justin's tone was reverent as he pulled her down again. "Ohh, Mother, don't leave me!"

In the premiere role of his life, Justin threw himself into a frenzy, tossing and turning, oblivious to Megan's rattled entreaties. Buffeted about in his viselike grasp, Megan longed to box his ears. Yet she certainly could not do such a cruel thing, which did not bode well for her escape. Gasping, she regrouped her energies and reviewed her nonexistent options.

Trying a new tack, she lowered her voice to a gentle cooing. "Yes, darling, this is your—ah—mother. Now be a good boy and let Mama go. I have some chores to

130

do. Mama will be right back, my love."

Little did Megan realize that she sounded like the most seductive mother alive. The Earl did realize it, and felt that his plans were beginning to get out of hand. With pure desperation, he redoubled his pleas. "No! M-Mother! Stay here—I don't want you to go!"

Megan rested a moment, hot and irritated. Evidently, her plan had not worked. Trying brute force again was hopeless—her "brute force" was rather useless against his. Exhaustion was creeping in.

"Mama?" The Earl queried pitifully. The pleading in his voice finalized Megan's surrender—that and an excruciating crick in her back. Touching his cheek lightly, she tried to reassure the delirious Earl. "Now listen, sweetheart, Mama is going to stay with you. Do you think you could be a good little boy and let Mama loose, just so I can shift a little?"

Within the next instant, before Megan could take it all in, she was shifted swiftly, firmly, and snugly, to Justin's side. Stunned, she lay there in confusion—how could a delirious man work so fast? A feat for a lucid man, it was a miracle for a feverish one. "Justin?" Suspicious, she tried to see his face; alas, he tossed his head to and fro, delivering his death moan.

"Mama?" Justin asked in fear.

"Yes, Mama—I suppose." Megan sighed and gave up. She patted him gently. "I'm here. Now go to sleep." Upon which, she promptly did.

Justin opened his eyes and smiled triumphantly into the dark. Hell would have no fury comparable to Meggy's if she ever uncovered his ruse. Yet the lady had been in need of sleep, and that was what she was getting—sleep. Inordinately pleased with himself and the world, he drifted off into slumber.

Megan slept soundly, the night's events an effective sedative. Justin, however, drifted, his wound awakening him occasionally. He was content though, surprisingly so. He gazed at Megan sleeping peaceably by his side, her silken hair lying across his chest. Unconsciously, he held her tighter. She cuddled closer in response. As her hand slid smoothly across his stomach to hold him tighter, Justin felt a familiar tensing.

Damn! He shouldn't be feeling these feelings. He should be too exhausted for that. Yet there they were. He most definitely was feeling them.

He studied the woman beside him. Besides the obvious attractions, he knew that it would be very special to teach her the ways of love. It unsettled him to realize how much he desired to be the one to teach her. He could not rid himself of the idea that, even in her inexperience, Meggy could teach him something about love, too.

Justin swore long and silently. What an absurd situation, and all of his own devilish design. He would not awaken her, of course. If his fading chivalry did not hold him in check, Meggy's green trust would.

Blast it! She was too open and innocent by far. She lay in a man's arms, blissfully sleeping away, as if he who lay next to her was not awake and was not harboring highly ungentlemanly desires. She simply was not up to snuff, totally naive about the defenses and wiles that protected her sisters. No one else would be quick to call her a kitten, but that was what she was, an innocent, trusting kitten. Confound it!

Chapter Nine

Awkward Awakening

Megan surfaced from her peaceful sleep. She snuggled closer to the warm, muscular body that embraced her. Breathing in a delightful male scent, she sighed like a contented kitten.

Before eagerly returning to her dreams, her eyes fluttered open briefly, then closed again drowsily. A moment more and they shuttered open in shock. That broad chest that pillowed her so comfortably was no dream! It was real, very real.

Megan's first reaction was to shoot from the bed, but that could only awaken the sleeping man beside her. Indeed, so entwined were they that it could only have served to topple them out of bed. The last thing she needed was to land upon the floor with the lucid Earl.

The fog of slumber fast retreating, she finally remembered the events leading up to her position next to Justin. "Faith, what a night." Embarrassed, she stared at the ceiling, afraid to look at her partner. Holding her breath, she very slowly and gently unwound Justin's arms from about her and sat up.

Justin did not stir.

Though last night had been perfectly innocent, a blush determinedly rose to Megan's cheek. Oh, how did she always land herself in these coils? Other delicately nurtured females passed whole lifetimes without ever involving themselves in such bumble-broths. What would Clare have done? That was easy, she would have swooned. Or, perhaps martyred sleep on the floor would have done the trick.

No, she refused to shoulder all the blame. It was the masquerade, and her grandfather's impossible will that had pitchforked her into these scrapes. Thus she blamed the one man who could not defend himself.

Heaven swiftly retaliated to this unfair accusation of the sainted dead; as Megan gazed intently upon Justin, his face patched with stubble, she gasped. Suddenly she knew, in no uncertain terms, the real reason for her various predicaments with this certain man. She was in love with him!

Megan's heart exploded in delight. It replayed the searing effects of Justin's kiss, flashed pictures of his humor-quirked smile, his wicked grey eyes, and his deep, teasing voice. Their fights, their companionable moments, and their laughter flooded her memory. God, how she loved him!

Her mind clamped down on her heart's ecstatic music. It cried in pain, aghast: "You are a fool, Megan! He does not love you!"

Justin's words surfaced into her mind. "If I needs must marry . . . might as well marry an heiress and get some blunt out of it . . . I want to go my own way after the wedding. I shall marry Megan Linton. Should I, Meg? . . . Maybe she'd like to stay in the country, and I could stay in town." And, the final axing of her budding love: "There is no such thing as marrying for love."

134

She slowly crawled away from the sleeping Earl and stood up cautiously. Turning, she looked with stricken eyes upon him. Even in sleep he exuded strength. Unable to resist, she bent quickly and kissed him lightly.

She straightened and squared her shoulders. Ignoring her rumpled dress—she had no intention of staying to change—she walked from the room, locking the door behind her. Today would be no different from any other day. She had many chores to accomplish, but attending a sorrowing heart was not one of them.

Later that morning, as she crossed from the barn back to the house with an important report on the prolificacy of the chickens, she stopped and raised her hands to shield her eyes as she made out a horseman approaching. He must have just left the house. She watched with a suspicion that swiftly crystallized into guarded wariness as the rider drew nearer.

Trenton Pavnor, spying on her, was galloping forward. Botheration, now what do I do? I have the devil's own luck! Her eyes lidded in speculation, she nevertheless presented a face of innocent surprise to Pavnor when he reined in before her. "Good morning to you, sir. What has brought you back to Argyle?" She was confident that it was her coquettish charm that drew him.

"I am looking for your master." He was curt, evidently in no mood to dally. "Surely a bit like yourself would know the whereabouts of your lover?"

"He is not my lover!" Megan retorted hotly before she could hold her tongue. She bit her lip in regret, studying Pavnor through lowered lashes. His eyes shifted nervously, betraying tension—perhaps even desperation? "Step softly, Meg," a voice inside her head whispered urgently. She forced a giggle and a conciliatory smile to her lips. "But I can tell you where

135

he is."

"Out with it," Pavnor ordered, a shade too eagerly. "Is he here?"

"La, no sir, he be in London town. He left two weeks ago and will return in two more." Megan relished the frustrated look on Pavnor's face.

"That is what the butler said—but what would he know? Now you, I think, would know better." Megan clenched her fists tightly, itching to slap the contemptible man's horse and send him flying. Yet a deep-seated caution held her in check, advising her to play along with him.

She frowned in assumed perplexity. "Why should I know differently? That is where he is!" She glared at him, setting her hands belligerently on her hips. "Here now, what's going on? He told me he was going only for business—something about horses! He ain't been lying, has he? Where is he? Who's he seeing?" She was very much the woman scorned.

"So you are his inamorata, my soiled dove." Pavnor smiled in smug satisfaction. Megan looked down guiltily, letting the silence paint her reputation black.

Pavnor snorted. He pressed his horse closer to her, and Megan had all she could do to steel herself to stand still. She refused to be intimidated by such a cur, though unbidden chills circled her spine.

"Where is he? Are you hiding him?"

"Hiding him? Why should I ever want to do that? I don't understand!" Megan's pitch rose like steam as she warmed to her role. "But if he ain't in London like he promised and is somewhere where he oughtn't to be, nobody will be able to hide him!"

Pavnor studied her dark, thunderous face through slitted eyes. Suddenly, he reached down and grasped her chin punishingly. He jerked her head up so that she could only see him. As she fell against his lathered

136

horse, he smiled cruelly into her astonished eyes. "So Justin has found himself a spitfire—how I would love to stay and break you in for him. But, sad to say, I do not have the time. But be warned, my little whore, if your master is not in London as you say, you will rue the day you were unwise enough to lie to me." Pushing her contemptuously aside, he spurred his horse onward with a crack of his whip.

Almost choking in repulsion, Megan determinedly shook off the dirty feeling his touch had engendered. Faith, Edward spoke the truth when he advised asking a man's name before kissing him. To think that she had ever kissed a toad like Pavnor!

Not that she planned to kiss many men in the future. Her arrogant master, for whom she had just accepted considerable insult, had somehow ruined the scheme of things where future romance or stolen kisses were concerned.

She stalked toward the house. Enough was enough. She intended to find out what was going on. Those Spaniards had had the right of it with the Inquisition, and she planned to borrow a leaf from their book.

Megan slipped into the kitchen first to deliver the happy news that the chickens prospered, news that greatly pleased Cook. Then, feigning weakness, she asked wanly if she could lunch in private within her room. Studying her taut, pale face, Mrs. Bodkins agreed, though her eyes widened considerably as Megan proceeded to pile high her sickbed tray with cold chicken, cheeses, and fruits. Megan smiled weakly, then staggered out of the kitchen with her burden.

Mrs. Bodkin and Cook discussed and worried over Megan's behavior for the next hour. They arrived at no conclusion, except that she had been in queer stirrups ever since Justin's and Edward's departures.

Megan, lugging her booty to her room, peeked furtively right and left down the hall. She laughed at such ferret behavior. Perhaps she could apply to Bow Street after her services were concluded here.

She then unlocked the door, no mean feat considering her burden. She kicked it open, then shut it behind her with another well-placed boot. Without glancing at the room, or the room's disturbing occupant, she waded over to the bureau and set the tray down in relief. She drew in a steadying breath before turning to face Justin.

Looking fiendishly handsome despite his rumpled, unshaved condition, Justin rested lazily upon his pillow, a disreputable sheikh. How unfortunate he looked so good, Megan sighed. With his free hand he held the brandy bottle, portraying the epitome of aristocratic boredom. But dancing lights twirled within his grey eyes as he looked at Megan. "Good morning, my dear—or rather, I must say, good afternoon. Did you sleep well, Meggy?"

"No, I didn't!" she said stoutly, despite the fact she had slept like a baby.

"I regret to hear that." His voice was worried but his eyes smiled. "Pray, was I so disagreeable as to snore?"

"No, that you did not," Megan admitted reluctantly.

"Never say I was blackguard enough as to steal all the sheets?"

"N-no, you shared the sheets." To deny it would have been useless, since they had slept so entangled as to not need a sheet.

"Well, that eases my mind considerably. Come, admit it, Meggy, I was a perfect bedfellow. And gentleman, dammit."

Megan, fighting recalcitrant fruit that threatened to topple off the tray at that moment, missed this. "I own you were a perfect—guest. But I refuse to be taken in by

138

this. I hope you know I am not one of your impressionable damsels."

"Ah, Meggy, Meggy! If you would but leave that food you are failing to manage, and come over here, I could prove you wrong. I'm sure an 'impression' could be made upon you if you would but let me." Justin grinned wolfishly.

"Indeed, I will not," Megan replied speedily, though she could not suppress an answering smile. She wagged a minatory finger at him. "Now, we will have no more of that my Lord. If you fail to behave, I will not serve you—perhaps starvation will keep you tame!"

"Do you truly believe that, Meggy dear?"

"No, I fear not." Almost sadly, she sat down on the bed with her tray. Justin looked up at her unwarranted soberness. Studying those serious, ocean-blue eyes, he wished suddenly that he could read her every thought. Today those eyes held a cloud within them and he wondered the reason.

"You were up and about early. How was your morning?" He ate the fruit, attempting to appear indifferent.

"Oh, vastly interesting. I hope you are not disappointed, but you missed a visitor this morning."

Justin stilled. "Indeed? Pray tell, who?"

"One of your favorites, I'm sure. Trenton Pavnor."

"Trenton! Damn! Surely you did not speak to him?"

"I'm afraid I had no choice. He hailed me just as I was returning from my errands. Evidently Crispins had refused him at the door."

"What did he say to you?"

"He seemed intent on knowing your wherabouts. He held the strange belief that you were here, rather than in London."

"I knew he'd reason it out. This is important, Meg—what did you tell him?"

139

"Why, that you were in London on business—horses, I believed. What else would I have said, my Lord?"

"Ha, good girl! Do you think he believed you?"

Megan considered that. "I rather think he did. Though I fear he is under the misapprehension that I am your present—ah—light-o'-love. You see, he was rather pressing on the matter of your location, and, hoping to appear as one who should know, I let him think what his evil mind had already believed. Indeed,you should have seen the pelter I fell into when he insinuated you were not in London, for I let him know you had sworn faithfully to me that you went to London on business."

"Capital, Meg!" Justin laughed. "You're a trump."

"And a fine actress, if I say it myself. I am pleased I could be of service—for some reason, I did not see you desiring a tête-a-tête with that man. He has a singularly unpleasant effect on one in the early morning." Megan stole a roll from Justin's plate, escaping the admonishing hand that slapped at her. After a few contented bites of the buttered tidbit, she licked her lips and went on. "Now, would you please inform me what all this cloak-and-dagger is about?"

"I'm sorry, Meg, that I cannot do."

"Cannot, or will not?"

"Will not," Justin apologized gently. "May I offer you some chicken?" He held out a cold, but savory, piece.

"Fie, Justin, you would stoop to bribery?"

"Without a doubt."

Megan sighed in exasperation. "Very well, odious man, I accept your 'fowl' offering." (Justin groaned in agony). "But I won't be put off for long. I'm not easily gulled or led astray."

"Never!" Justin agreed too heartily.

140

"Perhaps you could tell me why Pavnor is so hot for your blood, then?"

Justin studied Megan as she sunk her teeth prettily into the chicken. He sighed. He could not bring himself to lie to her.

"When we were young, Trenton and I fell in love with the same girl, as callow youths will. She was of genteel birth, but had little family to protect her. We vied for her attentions and soon it became a bitter contest. The poor girl was torn between the two of us—Pavnor can be charming when he chooses to be. One day, due to certain circumstances, he and she returned from a picnic by themselves. It wasn't to be far, and we thought everything would be proper. Well, his carriage supposedly broke an axle; they did not return until the next morning.

"Trenton had compromised her, whether by force or seduction I cannot say, but in a few months, it showed. Trenton boasted that surely he was the better man, but he would not marry her. In his eyes he had won the battle—he needed to do nothing else. She came to me in despair. She did not want marriage, bless her heart, only some idea of how to survive. I gave her an allowance and she now lives on one of my estates," Justin finished, lost in his memories.

"I'm sorry, Justin," Megan said quietly. "You must have loved her very deeply."

"I only wish I had." Justin spoke with true agony. "That is where the regret—and guilt—lies. My tender for her was mere infatuation spurred on by competition. She should not have had to suffer because of the rivalry between two foolish, selfish young men. If only I had known what Trenton was capable of!"

"But you didn't and couldn't. We are rarely aware of what we are capable of doing, let alone what others are capable of. And Pavnor's charm glosses over his cruelty," she added with a slight shiver.

"He did not hurt you?" Justin pinned her with a fierce stare.

"No, certainly not," Megan assured him quickly, misliking the unwholesome anger flickering in his eyes. "Now, my Lord, if you are finished with this feast, I will carry these remains to the kitchen." She laughed as she picked up the tray. "Poor Mrs. Bodkins and Cook, soon they will join with Uncle Josepheth in his clamor to see me safe inside Bedlam. I claimed illness, and then blithely toddled off with half the pantry."

"That should leave them at a proper standstill. You could have told them that you were eating for two, which would not have been a lie."

"Impossible man!" She eyed him sternly. His wicked grin proved her undoing and her tilted smile appeared. "Not enough that I might be carted off to the asylum because of you, now you would have me sent to a home for unwed mothers."

Justin chuckled. Suddenly, he could envision Megan with child. She would be beautiful. He shook his head to clear it. He was the one going insane! The stress must be taxing him more than he knew. He focused on her words. "Is there anything I can get you before I leave? Perhaps I should check your bandage?"

"No!" Justin roared. He did not know why he was reacting so crazily to Meggy, but he could not trust himself with her ministrations. Later, when he was back in form, he was confident he would not react like the veriest cub at her touch, but for the present, he did not trust her near him. "You forget, Meggy, that you are not the only person with medical skill." He wanted to erase the quick hurt that flashed in her eyes.

"Oh, yes, how remiss of me not to remember that you possess—ahm—medical talents." Megan hoped just as keenly to hide the hurt she knew was there. She strove

142

to expel the tension with a sally. "I'm sure Edward would tell me I should demand to see your other scar in payment for tending this new and future one."

As for easing the atmosphere, this sally failed miserably.

"No!" Justin exploded once again, feeling harried. Megan jumped at his vehemence, the chicken bones rattling on the tray. Try as she could to control it, hurt was welling up inside her. There was no pleasing the man!

She found herself staring into Justin's smouldering eyes. They glowed with a look Megan could not define. "Meggy, you play with fire. Don't tempt me!"

She swallowed, her eyes riveted to Justin's. Neither breathed. Justin was frozen, afraid that if he moved it would only be to cross and kiss Megan ruthlessly, merely to rid her of her stunned expression. She was like a poised doe caught at night in the light of a lantern.

He forced a smile. "I wouldn't wish to have you flying for the protection of your poker. Indeed, remembering the last intended aim of yours, I'd be afraid you might succeed this time. And if you threatened the future line of Argyle, I might be forced to sack you, then you would require employment—"

"Forcing me to become a Bow Street Runner," Megan finished, rather to herself.

"Beg pardon?"

"'Twas nothing, Justin, it is of no moment. Now I must go."

"Meggy," Justin said tentatively, "I will leave tonight—"

"Tonight! Oh, no you—"

"I am perfectly all right," he said firmly. "It is imperative that I leave this evening. Now Meg, don't bristle up—I will need your help once more. I fear

143

Argyle might draw some watchful attention from curious parties interested in my humble self."

Megan shook her head ruefully. "Explain no more. If you wish to behave so idiotically, far be it from me to cast the least rub in your way. If you wish to drag your wounded body into the night, I will arrange it!"

"I knew you could," Justin grinned, shifting more easily upon his pillow.

"Stuff. This is the last time you turn me up sweet, my Lord. I fully intend to have an explanation for this havey-cavy affair that you run. I claim that as reward for my services."

"A reward, Meggy? If we are speaking of rewards, let me give you a new dress." He eyed her ensemble with distaste.

"I like my dress," Megan ran a nervous hand over the sorry article. "All I desire is an explanation to this May game and nothing more." She left the room and locked the door behind her.

Justin chuckled to himself and reached for the bottle that Megan had discreetly moved away during their repast. He groaned when his wound objected. It had been a happy day when Meggy had come to work for them, he thought. He would have been in a sad pickle without her.

Justin slept the rest of the afternoon. He awoke when he heard the key grate in the door. He sensed Megan's entrance, but only opened his eyes when he felt her cool hand upon his forehead. "How do you feel?" she asked gently.

He had no intention of revealing the true state of emotion inspired by her sitting so close, her hand still smoothing his errant locks. "I'm fine," he replied curtly. "What time is it?"

"Somewhat about nine."

"Good God, I cannot believe I slept so much!"

144

"Neither can I." Megan cast a knowing eye toward the drained brandy bottle.

"I was bored to flinders!"

"It appears so. Meanwhile, while you have been—sleeping—I, your faithful servant, have been exercising my considerable talents." Justin raised a doubting eyebrow. "I, my Lord, have had Jed unobtrusively patrol and observe the area all day for any shady characters or happenings."

"Jed—unobtrusive! Not even slightly possible! In fact, are you sure you can trust him?"

"Of course I can trust him! He has been with—" Megan swallowed her words before she could say he'd been with her for years. "He's been trustworthy for as long as I have known him."

"Which means not a thing. As they say, love is blind!"

"Not this time," Megan said ominously. Her jaw tightened like a bulldog protecting his bone.

"All right, I cry quits." Justin raised his hand in defense. "Anything you say, Meggy. I'm sure Jed is all that is amiable—he just appears a dolt. That he has no more sense than a game pullet has no bearing, either, I am sure. You say love isn't blind, but it surely must if you don't think you'll commit homicide a month after the banns."

"He is not dull, merely loyal," Megan retorted with asperity. "A severe drawback in your eyes, I'm sure!" She paused, grasping the reins on her runaway temper. "This conversation leads us nowhere. Justin, believe me, Jed can be relied on. Now, he said that strangers had posted themselves not far beyond the woods. They loped off at about six and have not returned."

"Excellent. But we can't be positive they truly left, or that the watchdog fiancé detected them all."

Megan smiled with satisfaction. "I have considered

145

that, though I do not know who they might be. Therefore, I have secured you these!" Triumphantly, she pushed a greasy, rough bundle into his arms.

Justin's patrician nose quivered in distaste at the rank odor rising from the mass. His black eyebrows rose even further. "And what, pray tell, Meg, are these atrocitities?"

"Those, my lord," Meg giggled, "are your clothes. I do not wish to add to your conceit, but you are a highly recognizable person in those duds of yours. Not that you are a dandy or a fop," she conceded graciously.

"I am so glad you noticed."

"Yes, but anyone could tell you're a swell." She took pride in employing the new words she had gleaned from Jed this afternoon. "I imagine, however, that no one would recognize you in these."

"Good God, I sincerely hope not!"

"I thought it an excellent idea!" Megan replied, hurt.

"In other words, my well-meaning maid, the peacock without his feathers—"

"—will look like any plucked chicken."

"You leave a man very little dignity, Meggy!" Justin's shoulders shook silently. "Let us make a pact. I promise to remain properly humble, if you will but refrain from likening me to a plucked chicken."

"Whatever you wish, my Lord. Though you must admit, Justin, it will lend you a new view on how the other half lives. Ahm—we working class," she added quickly, hoping to sound more like a member of that group.

"I see that you are enjoying every minute of this," Justin complained as he swung himself up and off the bed.

"What are you doing?" Megan squeaked as Justin reached for his belt.

"Why, changing my feathers."

"Oh . . . well . . . of course. One moment!" She spoke quickly, for Justin was continuing the process. "I—I'll be outside and awaiting you. You can tell me when you are finished!" She dashed out the door, slamming it shut behind her.

She leaned against it, attempting to catch her breath. Suddenly she felt very foolish. She looked up and down the hall—a fine picture she would make if someone happened past to see her waiting outside her own door like an impatient visitor. She put her ear to the door only to draw back indignantly. He was chuckling!

Insufferable man!

She put her ear to the door again. Now he had fallen to humming. Megan sighed. She had gone and fallen in love with a loony.

Just at that sobering moment, the door opened inward without warning. Megan fell forward and would have fallen to the floor if Justin hadn't caught her. Flustered, she righted herself, ignoring Justin's knowing laugh. She looked up to glare at him when her jaw unhinged itself, leaving her with a decidedly flabbergasted expression. Megan had planned for Justin to look like a farmhand. Instead, with his dark looks and proud carriage, he appeared a rakish gypsy or marauding pirate.

"Well, madame, what do you think?" He reached over and gently tapped Megan's jaw back into its normal position. "An excellent fit, I'd say."

Megan cleared her throat. "Ahhm . . . it must suffice."

"Well then, no time to loiter. Step to it, wench." Justin strode past her toward the kitchen and its back entry. Megan, disgruntled, followed unwillingly. She scrutinized his walk and said hesitantly when they

147

reached the kitchen, "Justin, could not you—um—perhaps alter your walk, only slightly?

"Alter it? In what manner?" His eyes sparkled; he snapped with a barely concealed energy.

"Perhaps to a—well, a farmhand—shuffle, I'd say. You walk much too arrogantly, you know?"

"Indeed? I had never realized it!" He was enjoying Megan's discomfort. "Is this what you would wish?" He slouched forward glumly, losing a good two inches of height, capped his dark locks with a floppy, worn hat, and shuffled on laconically.

Megan's face took on utter delight at his change. "Oh, indeed, Justin, that is exactly what I had imagined. Goodness, where did you ever learn that? You are an excellent actor!"

"What, this? It was singularly easy—I merely bethought myself of your beloved fiancé."

"Oh, what an uncivil thing to say, after all Jed's help. But I refuse to come to daggers drawing with you."

"Yes, missus, just so, missus." Justin spoke with a gutteral country accent, touching his forelock obsequously.

"Well, begone with you, you lout." She was happy to play along. "The way should be clear—Jed was to warn me if not. He will be awaiting you with a cob."

"Thankee. I'm much obliged to ye, missy."

"Oh, do quit funning!" Megan opened the back door and after looking out, pushed Justin toward it. But then she placed a restraining hand upon him. "Is this dangerous business, Justin?"

"I'm afraid it is, my dear."

"Have a care, my Lord."

"I fully intend to." He shot her a sudden, rakish grin and turned to leave. Then he halted, turned around, and stepped close to Megan. "Just for future reference, Meg, I don't in the least resemble a plucked chicken

148

when denuded of my feathers." With that, he pulled her to him for a lightning-swift kiss.

Megan stood dazed as he faded into the darkness and left. Still befuddled, she closed the door and locked it. A telling flush rose to her cheeks; indeed, she could not help but think that Justin might be right upon that matter.

Chapter Ten

The Fight

Megan once again lay upon her bed, her mind roiling with turmoil. She pounded her pillows savagely, growling with exasperation.

The Argyle air, she thought, must contain an odd humor that induced sleeplessness. She tossed onto her back and stared broodingly at the ceiling. Three days had passed since Justin's departure, with nary a word. She sighed gustily. Life would be infinitely more pleasant if Justin would make a push to cease his disconcerting jack-in-the-box appearances. The man always arrived unannounced and left unexpectedly. Faith, she would be happy if he would just take himself off to the continent. Then the rest of Europe could fret over him!

It lay beyond her why she should be so bluedeviled. She had singularly succeeded where many other women with less pluck would have failed. She had met the terms of her grandfather's will and was now a wealthy woman. Mr. Tothwell had sent a message through an exuberant Jed that her service was at an end. She had merely to return to Linton Manor and drop the odious Earl from her memory. Simple!

Yet, as a triumphant and well-cushioned heiress, why didn't she feel more enthusiastic? She should be leaping with glee over her success, rather than perversely tossing and turning over an absent here-and-thereian such as the Earl of Argyle.

Surely, as an intelligent peeress, it behooved her to pack her feather duster and leg it as fast as possible away from Argyle and its infuriating, moneygrubbing master.

Imagine! She could return to her idealistic life at Linton Manor, sleeping late if she so desired, and waking up to hot chocolate and breakfast in bed. No more drab dresses, but colors and silks and satins—and soaking in perfumed baths for hours.

Next, she would steal a march on the ton and discover a worthy, honorable man who would love her to the depths of distraction, the distraction being all on his part, of course. Then someday, down that rosy future's path, the Earl would accidentally meet her at a glittering ball—she, by then, the toast of the town. She would be on the arm of her enchanted blonde Adonis . . . and he on the arm of a fubbsy-faced, knock-kneed, squint-eyed heiress who would woefully lack even the spirit to say boo to a mouse. let alone an arrogant son-of-an-earl like Justin.

Knowledge of who she was would strike him like lightning and he would weep and nash his teeth, agonized that he could have married her, Lady Linton, rather than some addlepated, pudding-hearted miss.

Strangely enough, at this juncture, Megan intemperately threw her pillow across the room. Who was she fooling? She could air-dream all she wanted, but it signified nothing. The terrible fact was that Justin would never be there for her!

151

Even if she could, Megan possessed too much pride to buy him. Unfortunately, she also possessed too much love toward him to enter into a marriage of convenience. That road led to constant heartache.

Still, the weaker part of her insidiously suggested that she simply prolong her masquerade at Argyle, at least until Justin came home. She was her own Mistress, and if she was pleased to stay on, who was to say her nay? She didn't have any pressing engagements. Too tired to fight, Megan finally succumbed to this soothing voice, her frazzled wits relieved to sweep the nagging problem under the proverbial carpet. Why did she worry over it tonight? She could decide tomorrow or the day after that, or even the day after that. . . .

Turning to go to sleep, she realized she lacked a pillow. She got up and padded over to pick up that vastly misused item.

Hugging it for comfort, she suddenly froze. There was a noise! Could it possibly be Justin's returning in his nocturnal manner?

Her heart flitted to her toes and flip-flopped back to its original place. Her mind raced. Looking down deprecatingly at her nightgown, she shrugged impatiently. She could not waste time to change, she would investigate as was. Indeed, it was most likely only her imagination, and if, in truth, it was Justin instead, she did not intend to let him escape. She meant to come to points with him.

Megan slipped out of her room, listening closely. Faint sounds rustled from the back of the house. She tiptoed down the hall to the kitchen.

A sudden, wild shiver raced up her spine. Odd. Treading noiselessly into the kitchen she crossed it quickly and lit a taper that hung from the fireside. All was disappointingly quiet. She snatched an apple from the bowl of polished fruit on the table, a sorry consolation for her efforts, she thought.

In the midst of taking a healthy bite, Megan froze. Across the room, a doorhandle rattled. It turned slowly, and then the door opened. A grimy, burly man stepped forward and waved a lantern, imprisoning her in its light. The bit of apple choked painfully in her throat.

The man himself jumped within his freeze coat when he discovered a wide-eyed maid staring at him from behind an apple. He looked her up and down; suddenly he grinned a malicious, blacktoothed grin. It did nothing to enhance his already unfriendly mug.

"Cor, she's the mort we're looking for, men!" he blurted in a stage whisper, leering joyfully. He crossed and set the lantern on the table. Megan, still sputtering on her apple, quicky deduced that one, this was no chance-met petty thief and two, there were, most unfortunately, others. She highly doubted that the man carried on converse with himself.

She opened her mouth, preparing to scream the house down, only to vent a pitiful squeak. That pernicious bit of apple refused to be dismissed. Helpless, Megan followed her next best instinct—she egged the remaining portion of her apple at the intruder and nabbed him in the eye. He, to Megan's everlasting envy, let out a startled roar.

Excessively pleased with the results, Megan grabbed an orange and chucked it at him, catching him in the stomach. The fruit-battered assailant snorted in bull-ish rage and charged. Megan had just enough time to send off another apple; it ricocheted off his forehead but, to Megan's sinking dismay, did not impede him. She had stalled him enough, however, to finally swallow the unobliging piece of fruit.

Deeming surprise might be her only hope, she threw up her hands and flapped them wildly, producing a

succession of helpless, buffleheaded bleats. Her quarry
filled with masculine confidence at this properly hysteri
cal, feminine approach, rushed at her with his guard
insultingly low. To his extreme chagrin, the once
dithering female coolly stepped back and landed a
straight left to his unsuspecting jaw, ruthlessly follow
ing it up with an uncivil knee to his groin.

"Decidedly unfair, but efficient," Megan observed a
Blacktooth, a stunned look upon his phiz, doubled
over in unbelievable agony.

Megan was not one to let grass grow under her feet
she enforced this policy by rudely shoving the pained
assailant backward. He thudded to the floor, effec
tively out for the count.

"Darn!" Megan cried as she looked up to see another
ugly customer come crashing through the door. He
however, advanced more slowly since he was forced to
step over his groaning colleague. Megan's heart
plummeted to her feet. Surprise was decidedly out; the
ashen victim sprawled on the floor was testimony to
instil caution in the stoutest of men.

Her heart sank even further, to her toes, as two
more thugs pushed eagerly through the door. "This
is absolutely unsporting," Megan railed, though she
doubted these rogues would respect the finer points of
the Fancy.

She backed up slowly, her eyes glued to the rum
touch in the lead. Her backside struck the cold stone of
the fireplace and she cursed. Were fireplaces always to
be her nemesis?

"What the devil is going on here?"

"Justin!" Megan squealed, very unlike herself. Her
peripheral vision caught a glance of the Earl at the
entryway and her spirits soared. Her heart merrily
returned from her feet to her chest. "Thank goodness
Could you be so kind as to lend a hand, my Lord, I'm i

154

a bit of a fix."

The assailants paused a second, casting each other a leery eye. The gentry were sure queer ones, doing the pretty in the middle of a mill. Assured by each other that it was not their party with attics to let, they commenced to attack.

The lead lout rushed Megan. Quick to seize the moment, she greeted him not with the science of boxing, but with the long-held protector of women—she thwacked him over the head with a cast-iron skillet she had pulled from the fireplace. Her hand reverberated from the impact of skillet upon skull, a deeply satisfying sensation.

The man slowly revolved into a crumpled heap upon the floor. Megan stood over him in high expectation. Lacking insight, he attempted to escape on all fours; Megan cheerfully put a stop to that nonsense by thwacking him again, and he fell prostrate at her feet. "Excellent!" she announced as she studied her handiwork.

While Megan was vanquishing her foe with the skillet, Justin was working to unburden her of yet another of her tormentors. As tall as Justin and just as burly, the man closed in on him with superb confidence—everyone knew that quality folks were too soft for a decent fight.

Alas, he erred. Justin possessed a handy bunch of fives and the over-confident thug ran into an iron left, then a severe jab to his breadbasket. To his credit, he remained standing and delivered a shying punch to the Earl's nose.

Megan, her ruffian still quite motionless, happened to glance over at this time. She flinched at the blow. Grabbing up the folds of her nightgown, she galloped to Justin's defense, skidding to a halt and standing eagerly poised behind the bobbing man. In a fortuitous moment, she clanked the enemy on the head. Unluckily the man had been simultaneously ducking Justin's blow and the hit failed to ring true. The man groaned, however, and Justin, though aggravated, civilly backed away. "Meggy, leave off! This one is mine!"

"I'm so sorry," Megan replied contritely. No sooner had she offered the apology than strong, imprisoning arms clamped about her from behind. At the same time, Justin's battered assailant, taking advantage of the Earl's gentlemanly cessation, delivered a swift punch to the ribs. Justin groaned in pain. "A—good one, old chap."

"Thanks, gov!" the man beamed. Justin then tipped him a doubler and sent him to grass.

"Sorry about that, old man." Justin then turned to the next fellow.

Megan struggled desperately against her captor, who smelt terribly of garlic and sausage. She flailed her deadly skillet, but to no avail, her captor being the now much wiser and more wary Blacktooth. Grunting, he dragged her along. Megan's feet kicked the floor in ineffectual anger.

"Unhand me you misbegotten, spineless, thatch-gallows!" Megan proceeded to rake him down with the choicest of stable cant she had acquired in her short lifetime. It was a truly staggering presentation.

"Blimy!" The man was awestruck; he had never had the fortune to hear such detailed, expressive swearing from anyone before, let alone a female. Confounded, he nearly loosed the impressive virage. But the fear of what dreadful retribution she might mete out if freed held him in check—indeed, it spurred him to greater efforts.

Acknowledging the improbability of fighting free while being dragged ignobly backward, Megan reversed her efforts, sending her surprised assailant tripping when she suddenly pushed with all her weight in his direction. With Megan obligingly speeding him along, he crashed to the floor.

In the momentary lapse while Blacktooth wheezed desperately in an attempt to catch his wind, Megan scrambled off him. He caught her again before she could brawl any distance away. Spying a table leg near her, she dragged herself toward it, Blacktooth unwillingly drawn behind her. Finally reaching it, she clutched tightly.

Blacktooth quickly realized that Megan had no intention of deserting her table leg. He stood up, hoping to pick her up and thus shake her away. He tugged; Megan held to her table leg, a veritable limpet. He tugged anxiously once more, and Megan kicked out fiercely. Blacktooth, fearful of a repeat of his earlier experience, steered clear. He settled for catching her about the waist and inching her and the table across the room and to the door, to what purpose, only his frenzied mind could know. "Aw, come on, lady, give over!"

"Excuse me, my good fellow, perhaps I may be of assistance?" A soothing voice spoke from behind Blacktooth, and a gentle hand came to rest upon his shoulder.

"Thanks! She's a bloody barnacle!" Blacktooth turned gratefully around. His eager smile drooped into a horror-struck gape when, in the solitary moment of sight left to him, he viewed an over-large, over-enraged Justin grinning down at him with the most evil of smiles. His peepers were then blessedly darkened for him.

Blacktooth, now minus a few of his namesakes, spiralled to the floor for the second time that evening. He toppled onto Megan, who still clutched lovingly to her table leg, her eyes screwed vigorously shut while she mouthed a silent prayer.

Justin stooped and flopped the crumpled wreck away from Megan, then offered a hand to her. She, however, remained totally enraptured of her table, evidently too intent to discern the changing of the guard. Slowly she realized that the hands upon her were wondrously gentle and reassuring and that the voice which drifted through her trance was amazingly kind and somewhat familiar.

"Meggy, it's me. Now do be a dear and stop hugging that table so amorously. 'Deed, you must let it go, darling—I promise it will stay right there. Come now, I'm sure that can't be comfortable!"

Megan realized that Blacktooth could never be the possessor of such a handsome voice. Cautiously she peeked her eyes open to discover Justin gazing at her with the gravest of concern and absently tugging at her in worry.

"You can cease pulling at me, my Lord," she croaked through dry lips, slowly relaxing her frozen grip. "I feel as if I am taffy."

Justin barked a laugh in relief and set her down gently, patiently waiting while she unwound herself from about the table leg and stiffly crawled out. Slowly she righted herself. Looking around in dazed bewilderment, she gulped when she counted the four dark shapes that cluttered the floor. "Oh my!" Suddenly she flung herself at Justin.

He caught her up happily, wrapping his arms around her in consolation and burying his head in her tousled mane. He rocked her tenderly, as he would a frightened child, and whispered, "Shh, sweetings, it's all right. Everything is all right."

He stilled suddenly, perceiving that what he had thought were hysterical sobs were none other than deep, throaty laughs.

Justin gently, but firmly, tugged Megan's head back by pulling on the mass of golden hairs in which his hands had somehow entangled themselves. "Meggy?"

Blue eyes sparkled up at him while her gamin grin tilted itself victoriously across her bruised and battered countenance. "Oh, Justin, lud, what a mill! My Lord, you were absolutely superb! Indeed, you must strip to advantage!" (Megan borrowed that from her grandfather's sporting terms.)

"But Meggy, that is what I have been politely informing you of all this age." Justin pulled her litheness closer in a burst of triumphant enthusiasm. Megan's ribs came near to cracking, though she paid little heed to them, too heady over the victory herself. "You weren't so rubbishing yourself, Meg. Why didn't you tell me you boxed?"

"Oh, I only know a trifle of the science, in truth."

"And do you—strip to advantage?"

"Oh, you wretched man, will you never cease to amaze me? There are four deadly assailants scattered about this kitchen, all of whom you and I fought, and you only see fit to stand here and exchange flirtations! Fie, my Lord, what a sad want of character!"

"But Meg," Justin objected, "I merely display a finer sense of priorities than the common man. Who are these ruffians to me?" Justin snapped his fingers imperiously.

"Indeed, a home question, my Lord. Who are they?" Megan trapped Justin with a steady gaze, the slightest trace of fear marking her voice. "Justin, they knew who I was. That one with the black teeth, who smelt so frightfully of garlic and sausage, said that I was the 'mort' they were looking for."

Justin pulled back, studying her intently. "Are you sure?"

159

"Yes."

"Oh my God!" He cradled Megan's head against his shoulder, hiding his face from her. "Forgive me, Meggy, I'm sorry." They stood entwined a silent moment.

Justin's turmoil was a palpable thing between them. Megan held him all the tighter, as if she could draw it into herself and away from him.

"I am going to kill him." Megan lifted her head at Justin's utterance and studied him with worried eyes. His face was taut, his features severe. A chill ran through her at the sound of his voice, but she smiled gamely, raising a gentle hand to trace the bruise along his cheek.

"You look fagged, my Lord." She attempted to laugh lightly.

"I'd not say you look to be in fine fettle either, my dear. What ingenious reason do you intend to employ this time?" Justin asked, pointing tenderly to her bruise.

"Perhaps a door?"

"No, afraid not, a trifle too worn. Indeed, you're sure to catch cold at that one. You exhibit far too many bruises to come about them merely by running into a simple door—unless, perhaps, you had repeated the experience, which no one will swallow."

"Oh dear, as bad as all that? I fear it must be the stairs then—how very mortifying. Though I own I won't have the slightest trouble imagining it in the least. Faith, at this moment I feel confident that I could have easily taken in several odd flights."

"The devil! Are you sure you are all right?" Justin's hands immediately roved over her, as if they could detect any possible injury.

"I am perfectly fine," Megan assured him. "Though I must own that I stand here so prettily solely due to your

160

support." She frowned fiercely at this, for it was no small admission. Yet she could no longer pretend differently, her knees having cravenly turned to water the minute she became safe within Justin's arms.

"Ah, cruel Meg, how you've dashed all my hopes! Here I thought you were brazenly throwing yourself at me!" Justin smiled, his eyes wicked.

Megan halfheartedly cuffed the chest to which she was so tightly drawn. "Odious brute."

"Meggy, be warned, someday you shall pay for all the unkind, wounding things you've throw at my head." A pleasant smile warmed Justin's lips. Megan showed no fear at this, only blinking sleepy eyes and, a vague, foolish grin. "Poor chick, you're all pulled about. What am I thinking of?" Justin shifted her to one arm and reached with the other to right a chair that lay nearby. He eased her toward it, and she limply slid into it as if she lacked anything as terribly solid as bones. "Like a beautiful rag doll," he thought.

He crossed over to pick up the skillet that lay abandoned a few feet away. After a moment's consideration, he stepped over to the hearth and carefully selected a hefty poker from the irons. These he brought to Megan, who had followed his movements with curious but dazed eyes.

"Madame, I present your weapons. I go to seek help in clearing this rubbish away. Be pleased to keep the peace in my absence." Megan hugged the domestic weapons to her heart, smiling benignly, for all the world like the queen of the fireside hearth.

A discrete tapping sounded at the back door. Justin tensed. Eyes narrowed in consideration, he went to the door.

"If that is another one come to join his cronies, Justin, be pleased to inform him that it is well past retirement and I am no longer receiving tonight,"

Megan called groggily. The excitement just past was acting queerly upon her. She had achieved her victory and with the subsiding of adrenalin, she heartily desired nothing more than to crawl to her bed and rest her battered body.

Closing her eyes, she propped her head upon her poker and dozed. Movement of sorts wafted about her, but she did not care to open her eyes and observe it.

She awoke to gentle shaking. Raising her sleepy eyes, she looked into Justin's lightly amused ones. Blinking owlishly, she yawned indelicately and peered about her. There were no longer bodies upon the floor. "Justin—where are they?"

"Why, I had them cleared away, my dear. I didn't think you would miss them much. And it certainly wouldn't do to have Mrs. Bodkins tripping upon them come morning, would it?"

"Now Justin, you wrong the good lady. I'm sure she would not be discommoded in the least. Why, she'd merely have those oafs' heads for washing, for being so bold as to clutter her domain."

Justin considered Megan, who was enjoying her little joke excessively, giggling like the merest debutante. He hauled her peremptorily to her feet. "Come along, we are going to bed."

"Justin, will you never cease to think upon that subject?" She stumbled heavily against him. Justin thought that a rather harsh indictment, since she was the disheveled lady clinging so desperately to him.

"Shame, Meg, you do me a grave discredit. I simply wish to put you to bed, not to bed you."

"Oh, well, then, that's all right." A sudden flush rose to Megan's cheeks. "And I own I am most heartily glad. For though it grieves me to admit it, I appear to be in need of some assistance."

Justin put a steadying arm around her and together

162

they walked down the hall to her room. He opened the door and carried his fast-fading maid to her bed.

As he eased her down upon the bed, he drew back, startled when her eyes suddenly snapped open. A warning went off in his head—those bleary orbs held the most penetrating and determined of looks. Justin groaned, mistrusting Megan's next words.

"Justin, I want to know what happened tonight. Who were those men and what did they want? Why were they after me? And do not think you can wheedle me with some Banbury tale. I intend to hear the truth, so no shamming it." She clasped his arm firmly as if she half expected him to attempt an escape.

"Meg, you are burnt to the socket. Now go to sleep and I assure you I will explain all upon the morrow." Justin tried to soothe her even as he worked to loosen her grip.

"No, now! Or I shall bring the house down about your ears with my cries!"

"Meggy!" Her fierce expression caused him to laugh. "Do you have the slightest inkling of the punishment for blackmailing a peer of the realm, my little spitfire?"

"Fiddle, I don't care a rush for that," Megan said gruffly. "I refuse to be put off. Just think how it would look—in my battered condition, they might very well believe me instead of you. Think of the scandal broth!"

A cursory inventory of Megan's swelling face and the various rents in her nightgown, not to mention her torn neckline, suggested the truth of Megan's words. Gads, but she was a sorry sight! "You really are an unprincipled piece of baggage, aren't you? All right, I admit defeat." Justin raised his hands in surrender. "This is not the best of bedtime stories, though—be a good girl and do get under the covers."

Megan obeyed dutifully. Justin arranged her blankets and settled more comfortably upon the bed. He

163

smiled at her avid interest and looked down at his hands. "As you must now be aware, I perform diplomatic services for the government. One day they called on me and explained that secrets were filtering out and they believed they knew the culprit. They were, however, having a spot of trouble in catching him, for though they knew who he was, any quick movement on their part would scare him off, our culprit being the cautious type.

"Though they knew it was not really in my line of work, they asked if I would do the investigating, for the criminal operated in the area of my county seat. They deemed I would be the one most able to observe him and to rouse the least suspicion so doing—which stands to reason, for I have never been considered an agent of that sort."

"That is why you came here!"

"Yes. It would not be unexceptional if I were to visit my estate. It was a simple task to make Mother decide that she wished to visit Argyle Court. As skitterwitted as she is, she soon assumed that it had been her idea." There was a fond chuckle from Megan at that; Justin answered with a grin.

"So that explains it all," Megan said to herself. It was not so wondrous that Mr. Tothwell's well-studied plan had come a cropper. His logic did not stand a chance against the abritrary movements of Lady Augusta and her son.

"Explains what?"

"Oh . . . nothing. And who was this spy—don't tell me, I know. It must have been Pavnor."

"You hit the nail on the head. Now you can see why I was not loath to accept the assignment."

"Ha! You must have been in high alt," Megan said.

"Come, Meg, certainly you are not implying mine is a vengeful nature? Though I own that this assignment did attract me. At first, however, I was hobbled, for

164

though I had come here, I still did not know how to observe him closely, Pavnor and I not being the closest of friends. Inviting the locals to the ball helped a little, but Pavnor must still have smelt trouble, for his activities lessened considerably with my arrival. That is why the department called me back to London. They reasoned if it was set about that I had quit the area, Pavnor would resume his activities. In truth, I did not leave for London but remained here to investigate. Not getting tired are you?" Justin asked suddenly.

"Oh no, I find it vastly intriguing—to think Pavnor had such intelligence."

"Oh, he has a very sharp brain. Lucky for us, it was not sharp enough. As sure as check, when he thought me safe in London he started up his system of spies and couriers. That last night I saw you, I had caught a courier and we had come to blows over his missive. Unfortunately, I heard someone coming, so I took his wallet and belongings as well, hoping to mislead them into thinking me a mere petty thief. In taking that time, however, one of them had the chance to come upon me and get a swipe with his knife—worst of all, both men could have recognized me.

"Run off my legs, I doubled back here, with them on my heels. That was why I demanded that no one know I was here. If Pavnor knew it was I who had taken the missive, and not just held it in doubt, I'm sure he would have folded his game and left the country. He had a major deal that was to take place over in Lancaster. We must have lulled his suspicions—for which I have you to thank—for he was reassured enough to attempt the exchange. That is why I left you in such a hurry that night—we had much to do to be able to catch him at it. That night, however, we were successful in capturing all his men."

"His men? You didn't catch him?"

"Meggy, please, you must break yourself of this

habit of interruptions before a story is told. No, we did not catch him immediately. You wouldn't have faced this dreadful evening if we had. Trenton managed to escape from us, though we had him down until he pulled a gun at the last minute. Pure mismanagement on our part. He did escape, and evidently comprehended that I was indeed involved."

"Good Lord, he told me I'd be sorry if I lied to him."

"Yes, strange—you pinched me off about my strong sense of revenge, but Trenton must be the master of it. Though he was wise enough to fly for the coast, he still took time to pay some cutthroats to come and attack you—most probably intended them to do me in as well. We'll have it from those fools, no doubt, when they wake up."

"Where are they?"

"Oh, I had the servants take them down to the gaol."

"Oh. I suppose this will seem incredible to me on the morrow, but now that I know what transpired, I am ready to go to bed. I can only say I think it excessively sad that Pavnor got away."

"Oh no, my love." Justin's eyes gleamed down at her. "As I've said, you should not interrupt me. While we were clearing the kitchen, a messenger arrived with the tidings that Pavnor had been caught at Dover."

"Oh Justin, how famous!"

"Somehow, I knew you would approve. He will pay, Meggy—I will see to that—not only for betraying his country but for sending assailants against you."

Megan smiled drowsily and placed her hand upon Justin's clenched ones. "They did not succeed, due to your timely intervention. I am deeply grateful to you for that. And think, I did get to see my first mill!"

Justin laughed. He unclenched his fists and smiled at Megan. Her tawny hair haloed her head while her ripped neckline, unattended, slipped to display an alluring expanse of smooth, creamy skin and gently swelling breasts. Justin watched as Megan's eyes dilated, hopelessly trying to stay open. "Go to sleep, Meg. All's well that end's well." He leaned over to proffer a quick kiss—yet when he met her warm, tender lips, he did not draw back.

Megan, half-asleep and half-awake, responded naturally—for dreaming, that is. Her arms slid around him and she kissed him fully. He enwrapped her, slightly lifting her off the pillow to hold her soft body closer. She arched against him languidly, and her hand fluttered through his hair.

Leaving the sweetness and passion of her lips, Justin tenderly kissed her closed eyes and bruised cheeks. Then, with feather kisses, he seductively traced her neck and shoulders. Megan sighed and her head fell back. She sighed again—only this time, it sounded strangely like a snore. Justin suddenly peered at her, astounded. She had fallen asleep!

This time Justin sighed. He laid her back upon the pillow, drew the covers snugly about her, and gently pushed back a few errant tendrils of hair that had strayed across her face. He sat and gazed upon her for a few quiet moments.

"What, pray tell, am I to do with you, my dear? I fail to recall when I have ever met such a female to dampen my consequence. Ah, the blows you render to my assurance. I imagine it would be beyond hopeless to tell you that most young ladies do not fall asleep when in my arms? Indeed, I disremember when one has."

There was no answer forthcoming.

"Ah, I suppose not." Justin bent and kissed Megan's forehead. He stood and walked to the door, but turned at the threshold. "Good night, my dangerous kitten. Sweet dreams."

Chapter Eleven

Further Contretemps

Justin slept the sleep of the exonerated and awoke late that morning to set about his ablutions cheerfully. As he indulged in the luxury of shaving himself, his mind reviewed the energetic evening just past.

He came near to cutting himself when a sudden chuckle escaped him, for the vision of Meggy in her ridiculously virtuous nightgown, flailing her skillet with unprincipled abandon, had come to mind. Oh, the look on that clobbered ruffian's face!

He wiped his face clear of lather and went to find a fresh linen shirt. He slipped into it, crossing to the window as he did up the cuffs. Drawing the curtains open, he blinked at the young sun's excessive exuberance. His eyes teared, but after they accustomed themselves, they focused on a man running toward a woman in the yard; the man was obviously a groom and the woman a maid. As the groom reached the maid, he grabbed her and swung her in dizzying circles. Halting in embarrassment, he set her down, looking terribly sheepish.

"Ah," Justin mused indulgently. "Young love!"

Unexpectedly, the Earl's dark brows met in frowning conference over a quivering noise. Hold! That laughing maid was Meggy! That over-demonstrative lout was his groom Jed!

Justin snorted grimly as he observed Jed shyly offering Meggy a note. Meggy took it and opened it, smiling up with her winsome grin at the hovering, oversolicitous groom. Justin cursed and turned from the window. The great lummox had probably written her some drivelling piece of misspelled poetry.

Anger flooded through Justin as a nauseating vision of Jed's rough hands caressing Meggy presented itself. Blister it! What did Meggy see in that clumsy clod? She, the woman who had fallen so swiftly and unflatteringly asleep within his arms, offering herself and her life to that peasant!

Could she not see what folly she was committing? The plodding Jed would never be able to understand, let alone appreciate, her spirit and effervescence. He could never be able to support or guide her. And if he was so foolish as to try, he could only drag Meggy down. Damn the galling presumptuous puppy! Damn Meggy!

Eyes ablaze, Justin slammed out of his room in a combustion of rage, his shirt unbuttoned and flapping wildly. He charged smartly down the steps, through the house, and into the kitchen. "Mrs. Bodkins!"

"Eeks! Glory be!" Mrs. Bodkins turned from the fire to find herself cornered. Her hands fluttered to her chest as Justin advanced towards her with the darkest of expressions. She gulped as she became cognizant of the fact that his Lordship was not presentable; his shirt flapping open displayed an alarming expanse of chest.

"Lord love ye!" Mrs. Bodkins blushed, looking anywhere but toward him. "Ye frightened me to death.

For a moment, I thought you were a ghost."

Ignoring her justifiable meanderings, Justin pinned her with a black look. "I will have a bottle of brandy in my room within the instant!"

"Why—why certainly, my Lord—oooh," she moaned, as she finally braved looking into his face. "What happened to ye? Your face! Oh, my poor bairn!"

"Never mind that! Send me Meggy with the bottle of brandy! No one else, do you understand?"

Mrs. Bodkins jumped at this request. "Wh—what was that, my Lord?"

"I said, send me Meggy. I expect the wench and the brandy in my room within the nonce. I do not care where you find her or with whom you find her, just find her!"

"But—but, Master Justin!" Mrs. Bodkins eyed his open shirt; it had taken on an undertone of menace. "Ye shouldna' be askin' a young lady to your rooms!"

"I'm not asking any young lady anything! I—am—ordering—Meggy to bring me brandy. I demand her now or there will be hell to pay!" With that, Justin stormed out.

Mrs. Bodkins stared in bafflement after the rampaging male. Begorrah, the man had gone daft! What did he want with brandy so early in the day? And demanding that Meggy bring the loathsome brew, with him all unclad!

Her whirling mind had but a second to right itself before Megan, blithely unaware, stepped into the room. Mrs. Bodkins groaned at the sight of her face. "Oh no, not you too!"

"What is that you say? Isn't it a delightful morning?" Megan delivered the words as enthusiastically as she could, then halted in concern as she heard gurgling sounds erupting from the stricken housekeeper. "Please, Mrs. Bodkins, don't look so! Here, take deep

170

breaths! I promise it only looks bad. I had an—an accident, 'tis all. Please tell me my face isn't so frightful. I made sure the powder would cover it."

"Ah no lass. Ye just took me by surprise. Where—where did ye come by that face?" Mrs. Bodkins strove hard for calm.

"I . . . so skitterwitted of me . . . I fell down the stairs last night."

"The stairs—last night?" Mrs. Bodkins moaned. She succumbed to a most unhappy conclusion. "Oh, why did ye do it, lass? To be sure, Master Justin is a tempting one, but how could ye?"

"How could I what?" Megan asked, utterly confused.

"How could—how could ye go and throw your cap over the windmill with Master Justin?" Mrs. Bodkins asked in a rush, wringing her hands.

"What? Throw my cap—with Justin? No such thing! Why, however did you come by such an—outrageous notion?"

"What were you doing last night—upstairs?"

"Upstairs? . . . Ah . . . well . . . you see, I . . . heard noises! And I thought to investigate. It seemed to come from the second floor. I didn't discover anything out of the ordinary . . . but when returning, I tripped and fell down the stairs. It is wondrous that I didn't waken the whole household. It was terribly mutton-headed of me—I'm frightfully fiddle-footed at times." Megan offered this up with a conciliatory smile.

"Praise be to the sainted mother! Will yer ever forgive me, lass?" Mrs. Bodkins apologized contritely. "I can't think how I could have thought such a—a scatterbrained thing. But what with Master Justin actin' the way he did, what was I to think?"

"Indeed, I would have thought the same," Megan agreed bracingly. "But in what way was Master—Lord

171

Devenish acting? He has returned home, I gather?"

"Aye, that he has. And did he give me a terrible start! He came a-tearin' in here—and he wasn't dressed."

"What?"

"'Tis the God's honest truth, dearie. He came chargin' in here lookin' like the very devil, and with his shirt all undone! Though me laddie does have a brawn chest, mind ye," Mrs. Bodkins was sure to add. He might be deranged, but Justin was still her favorite lunatic.

"Oh, is that all?" Megan sighed in relief.

"Is that all! Why, the man was lookin' like sin and actin' like insanity! Oh, and his poor face! It looked like it could have been cousin to yours—and he ordered brandy, mind ye, this early in the morn! And said that ye was to bring it, no one else would do! Or there would be hell to pay!"

"He said that?" Megan asked, perplexed. "How strange. Well, we best do our master's bidding—though it stumps me why he was so determined I bring his drink."

"It has me fair betwattled," Mrs. Bodkins admitted, calming down in the face of Megan's commonplace manner. "Though I don't think I should send ye. I don't like it above half, Master Justin being in such a mood that he was."

Megan gave a delighted laugh. "Indeed, he must have been, to send you into a pelter. Never say that you mistrust your very own laddie? Do you think he'll go beyond the line?"

"Now don't ye go roastin' me!" A slight smile finally lit her face. "You're always the one to make me laugh. And to be sure, I've just been so overset this morn, what with Master Justin actin' as queer as Dick's hatband and both of ye walkin' about with such faces. I must have slipped me moorings for a wee while."

"Yes, I'm sure it is enough to send even the strongest into high fidgets," Megan said. "And for my part, I'm frightfully sorry to have worried you so. And as for Just—Lord Devenish—I'm sure it was merely the strangest of humors. He must have just arrived from London, and perhaps the journey was infelicitous."

Megan went to the cellar and returned with a bottle of brandy. "Now, don't go fretting yourself to flinders. Just sit down and let me take care of this for you. In truth, we don't want to pay 'Hell' for the mere pleasure of disobeying Lord Devenish do we? Faith, I've done that countless enough times in the past to know!" Megan winked, smiled her mischievous smile, and waved goodbye.

Megan hummed happily as she went up the stairs, tray in hand. What could Justin want? Perhaps he had received more information about last night's happenings.

She had already received uplifting information from Jed that very morning. In fact, he had been so excited with the news as to have picked her up and swung her around. Mr. Tothwell had sent word that they could leave today and that he would await them in town that afternoon. She planned to send Jed back; he was longing to return to Linton Manor and his true fianceé, Mary Lukins.

As for her—well, she would meet Mr. Tothwell, but only to inform him that she intended to remain behind at her post. She had far too many goodbyes to make to walk out without warning. Exactly when she planned to depart, she didn't know, but she could decide that another day.

She tapped lighly upon Justin's door and heard his brusque command to enter. She smiled to herself, her mind flashing back to that one rainy night so long ago. Pushing open the door, she carolled, "Good morning,

Justin. Isn't it a marvelous day?"

Her eyes eagerly circled the room until they rested upon Justin. His back was turned to her and he stared out the window. Studying his straight, arrogant stance, a loving smile twitched at her lips. She trod silently to the table and set the tray down.

"Here is your brandy, Justin. Though it was touch and go whether I would be permitted to deliver it to you. Faith, did you know you sent poor Mrs. Bodkins into a rare taking? Lud, she was overset! She informed me, mind you, that you tore into her kitchen undressed! Shocking, Justin, positively shocking!"

"That is quite improper talk, ma'am," Justin bit out from over his shoulder.

Megan stilled. Forsooth, she knew that tone! It appeared that Justin was in full temper after all. Now what had she done to set his back up this time?

"Mrs. Bodkins did relent," Megan offered pleasantly, "so here we are, the brandy and I. Did you have anything you wished to discuss with me?"

"You are a fool, Meggy," Justin condemned coldly.

Megan breathed in sharply at this frontal attack. "And this failing is what you wished to discuss with me? Well, perhaps you are right, who am I to pluck a crow with you, but I do feel that you're coming it a bit too strong. I mean, I've been called a zany before, and an original, and even hoydenish—but a fool, Justin? Must it come to that?"

"You are a fool!" Justin cut back.

"My Lord, " Megan said, "I certainly do not wish to set myself at loggerheads with you, especially so early in the day, but could you be so kind as to explain why you have arrived at this rather sweeping decision? I don't wish to appear behind hand, but last night you were well-pleased with my behavior. What has occurred to change your mind? Upon reflection, I own

174

that the skillet was slightly unconventional, but I wouldn't call it foolish, for it seemed to turn the trick." In fact, she thought ominously, if she only had that lovely item now, it might serve to do the trick nicely once again.

Her thoughts were perhaps stronger than she knew, for at that instant, Justin swiftly turned around, his face a mask of cynicism. "I am not talking of last night. I refer to your affair with that nodcock groom."

"What?" Megan asked. What had set him off on that tangent? Of all possible causes for his vexation, her groom Jed had never entered into her thoughts. Her mind, however, did grasp one significant word, and since any place seemed a likely place to start, she latched onto it.

"Affair! With Jed! Well, I believe you have finally lost a tile. I mean—just because he is my fiancé does not mean that we've—we've 'known' each other," she said with as much dignity as possible.

"Don't try to deny it! I had the priviledge of witnessing your rendezvous this morning!"

Megan sighed, almost in relief. At least she knew from whence the attack originated. She was shocked out of her contemplation, however, by Justin's next words.

"If I were you, I'd ensure he was safely buckled before I—"

"Before I what?" Megan demanded indignantly. Then her eyes widened in comprehension. "Well of all the ramshackle things to suggest!"

Her temper, after the fraying of last night's excitements, was not at its best. She advanced on him angrily. "Zounds! A simple meeting a yard hardly portends a love affair! At least not in my book, though I have doubt that in yours, it does. Faith, I'm sure an open fairway would suffice for you. But, alas, I am not

175

so broad-minded. I hold much higher standards of the proper locations for conducting illicit meetings. I prefer the more secluded and romantical."

"There! You admit you meet for rendezvous! You admit you aim to meet with Jed!"

"I admit no such thing! Oh, this is infamous!" Suddenly Megan's eyes took on a reckless glint and she said with fine dramatics, "Oh, pray, do forgive me. To rip up at you so ungraciously when 'tis clear you only have the kindest intentions for my welfare. How illmannered of me. Indeed, after calmer thought, and studying it in the light you have presented, I see that you are in the right of it. Indeed, the best thing for me to do is follow your fine counsel and marry the nodcock— I mean Jed—as speedily as possible. God forbid that passion carry us away before the vows are read! Or worse yet, that he escape my clutches altogether. Oh yes, thank you! I will set the banns this very day!"

Justin stared at her in impotent rage. He perversely cartwheeled in his philosophy to express an exceptionally progressive view. "No! I would rather you had an affair with that noddy than see you riveted to him for life. Though there are far better men than he for such!"

"Oh, do make up your mind, my Lord! Which is it to be, mistress or wife?"

"Mistress!" Goaded beyond endurance, Justin cared very little what he was saying.

"I am deeply indebted to you for your kind advice. Since I am now to set foot on the path to becoming a mistress, rather than anything so commonplace as a respected wife—for I live only to oblige you, of course—perchance you could offer some further advice upon whose mistress I should become. I mean, Jed is out, he could never offer me the elegancies of life that I could command—so that leaves me at a stand. Whose mistress should I become?" Megan purred, her eyes slitted in feline anger. "Is it your mistress I should become, Justin?"

"No!" shouted Justin, all the more fiercely because a deep, integral part of him desired nothing less than that. He squared his shoulders, however, and looked down arrogantly at Megan. "I do not enter into affairs with the lower orders."

"I know, I know. How often you repeat yourself. Perhaps you subscribe to redundancy as an acceptable form of conversation, but I find it decidedly flat. And do permit me to inform you that I, my stiff-rumped, top-lofty Lord, would never demean myself to become your mistress, even if you were the last man on earth and I was starving in the streets. I, sirrah, do not have affairs with the upper orders! They are arrogant, selfish, hypocritical prigs!"

"Prigs? Ha! No, you prefer callous clods who would either beat you senseless or bore you witless!"

"Jed would never dare to harm me," Megan retorted. "He is a gentle, honest man!"

"Man?" Justin sneered. "Don't be so incredibly naive, Meggy! If that puppy is your idea of a man, you are vastly mistaken in what one is." He advanced upon Megan and roughly grasped her arm.

Megan jerked back, suddenly and unaccountably afraid of Justin's uncontrolled rage. She trembled at his touch, feeling his coiled anger shooting through her.

"Let me go, Justin," she said as coolly as possible. "And I will forget we ever held this conversation."

"No, Meg, I fear I cannot allow that," Justin said gently, even with regret. His voice then deepened against her plea. "I won't ever let you forget!"

Slowly and relentlessly he drew her toward him. Reading his full intent, Megan began to struggle fiercely as he forced her hands behind her back.

He kissed her in controlled, harsh anger. She was forced to submit, in reluctance and caged fury. Yet, suddenly—betraying both combatants—such unworthy passions ignited into a demanding gentleness.

Justin, who had bent Megan ruthlessly to his form, slowly released her wrists in order to mould her tenderly to him. Megan's hands, freed, slid tentatively to his shoulders to sway him to her will. The kiss deepened and sweetened, yet Justin drew back, aghast to find that he kissed Megan's eyes and lips through salt tears. His darkened eyes stared at her in burning consternation. "Meggy?" he whispered hoarsely.

The naked pain shimmering in Megan's eyes stabbed at him from her ravaged and vulnerable face. Megan, hurt, struck out like a wounded animal. She swung back and slapped Justin with all the weight of her pent-up emotions. Justin's head snapped back from the force of the blow. He stood there silently.

"Don't ever dare to touch me again, my Lord," Megan said with deadly calm. Turning, she walked from the room, straight and regal.

Justin blinked as the door closed, blocking out the sight of Meggy. He stood transfixed. Finally breaking from his trance, he strode to the table and threw himself into the chair. He poured a glass of brandy and swallowed it in one gulp.

He stared across the table to the empty chair where Meggy had once sat, on a rainy night so very long ago. He looked at the door from whence she had left. "Damn you, Meggy, damn you to hell!" He reached for the bottle.

Megan shut the door to Justin's room, one racking sob shaking her. She caught herself up sharply. "Justin is right, you are a fool. A romantical, little fool."

Resolutely ignoring her burning pain, Megan walked down the stairs, head held high.

Well, she might be the fool that Justin claimed, but she was still Lady Linton, and no man would be allowed to tear her apart so—at least no man would ever again. She walked silently to the kitchen, knowing the course she would take.

Mrs. Bodkins looked up from her cooking to see a subdued Megan enter, a slight stain of tears upon her cheeks. "Ah, my poor lass, what has happened? What did he do to you?" The fact that his Lordship was referred to as 'He' did not bode well.

Mrs. Bodkins bustled over to Megan, and with tender clucks, gently directed her to a chair. Megan sat down stiff and rigid. She attempted a reassuring smile that wavered into a pitiful quirk. "It's not much, we merely came to cuffs again."

"About what, dearie?"

"Oh—a trifling matter!" Megan waved it away, her eyes pleading Mrs. Bodkins not to inquire further.

"I see." Mrs. Bodkins nodded noncommittally, nobly stifling her curiosity. "And did he turn you off?"

"No, faith, that is the one thing he failed to do," Megan retorted wryly. She drew in a shaking breath. "But that's neither here nor there, for I intend to leave this afternoon."

"Leave!" Mrs. Bodkins exclaimed. "Ah no, lass, don't do it. Don't go that away. Surely ye can patch it up. Ye've set his back up 'afore and still come about right. Ye can do it again in a winking."

"No, not this time, I fear," Megan said weakly, dashing at a tear. "Oh, what a piece of work we are, making over nothing! It is high time I left—all the arrangements are in order—" Megan then eyed Mrs. Bodkins tentatively. "You were aware that I was to stay only for a time?"

"Aye, lass, that I was," Mrs. Bodkins sighed. "I'm not denying you have a right to leave, but don't ye wish to say goodbye to—everyone? We've all grown powerful fond of ye!"

"Yes, and I've grown fond of you—something I now have to reckon with." Megan's eyes blurred with troublesome tears. She blinked the dratted salt drops away and sat up stiffly. "But I can't face saying goodbye—it's more than my composure. 'Deed, I might never leave then, and what a pretty thing that might be!"

"That wouldn't be half bad, the way I see it," Mrs. Bodkins returned quietly. "Are ye sure ye must go?"

Megan looked at Mrs. Bodkins openly, her defenses down and the deep pain glimmering in her drenched ocean-blue eyes. "I've landed myself in an impossible coil. Matters are past repairing. If I could possibly change things, you know I'd not turn tail and run, I'd stay and fight. But things are not that way."

Mrs. Bodkins held her glance a moment, cleared her throat and nodded mistily. Sniffing and looking away quickly, she aided Megan in the only way she knew— she said not a word.

Finally, she broke the silence. "Aye, lass, I guess ye must leave then."

Megan smiled in heartfelt gratitude. "Please, Mrs. Bodkins," she begged, "do not inform anyone of my departure this noon. I know you do not know where I plan to go, and in truth, it is for the best. Do not try to discover it—I assure you I am going to a safe and sound . . . position." Megan laughed ironically, but her heart felt cold.

"Now lass, think on it before ye take this step. Arn't ye being a mite too harsh on the Master?"

"No," Megan said, drawing in a steadying breath. "Please acquit me of running off in a pet—it is no such

180

thing. I don't expect you to understand, but there is no possible way to rectify matters. Indeed, there is no reason for me to do so. His Lordship has made that painfully clear. Trust me, I know what I am about. At least," she added wryly, "I think I do."

"Nay, lass, I trust yer judgement," Mrs. Bodkins sighed. "I didn't mean to tease ye. I just wish this didn't have to be—I'm going to miss you."

"And so will I miss you. I couldn't have survived without all your kindnesses. I thank you from the bottom of my heart, Mrs. Bodkins, and I'll never forget it. But now," Megan said quickly, "I'd best get out of here before I make a complete cake of myself and turn into a watering pot."

Mrs. Bodkins sniffed loudly and choked out, "Goodbye, dearie. May God speed you!"

Justin remained shut within his chamber the day long. He supped deeply from man's solace against the tortures of womankind; in fact, he drank six bottles of solace. By noon he was royally foxed. By nightfall, he had shot the cat. Tuttle, his dapper and disapproving valet, put him to bed.

The next morning, head pounding and mouth fuzzy, Justin went to the morning room to partake of breakfast in a civilized manner. His bemused brain wondered what catastrophe had transpired to send every servant into the dumps. Justin felt he must be surely mistaken, but for a brief second, he believed he had spied a disapproving frown upon Crispin's basilisk face. What was the old duffer's problem?

The only one who appeared to be in fine fettle was Uncle Josepheth, who joined Justin at the table and, with blissful lewdness, proceeded to hem and haw over the ample charms of one of the local barmaids. Unable

181

to stomach Uncle's lascivious transports so early in the day, Justin escaped.

As he walked toward his room, he discovered servants scuttling from his path right and left. His head pounding too much to dare consider such bizarre behavior, he went by the kitchen to request another bottle of solace.

Mrs. Bodkins merely bobbed her head smartly and consented, without even the lightest of lectures on the evils of drink. In fact, she sent him up an extra bottle. Now, if Justin had not been in such a bad skin, this unusual behavior would have puzzled him. Today, however, he accepted the bottle without a question.

On the fourth bottle of the third day, Justin came to a momentous conclusion. He must make amends with Meggy. Even if she still held him in contempt, he could at least see her. That was the one thing he desired most, for the memory of her pain-filled eyes haunted him.

He would change that and erase the memory, making her laugh again. Yes, he would make her laugh again and make her take back all those cruel words of hers. Not that he would ever touch her again. He had simply lost his temper and control the last time. He fully knew the proper behavior between master and servant, and their kissing was decidedly out. No, he wouldn't touch her again, but he must see her!

Justin awoke the next morning with this firm resolve. He rang for Tuttle and proceeded to dress with more detail than if he were attending a royal duke. After two hours, he strolled from the room, a fine figure of a Corinthean. He left Tuttle, along with twelve neckclothes and three jackets, a crumpled wreck.

Justin wilfully attacked his breakfast and did justice to two eggs, four pancakes, a rasher of bacon, and three pastries. Crispin's eyes widened considerably at Justin's impressive intake, a truly wonderful performance after a three-day-old drunk. Well-sated, Justin pushed back his chair, cheerily bade Crispin a good morning, and went to find Mrs. Bodkins.

"There you are, Mrs. Bodkins, light-o'-my-heart," Justin called as Mrs. Bodkins went hastily spinning around a corner in front of him. She stopped reluctantly.

Justin's eyebrow rose at this obviously reluctant reception. Yet he had no time for household contretemps. "Send Meggy to me in the study. I wish to hold speech with her."

Mrs. Bodkins paled and clutched convulsively at the linens she held.

"I—I'm afraid that I c-can't, my Lord," Mrs. Bodkins stammered, raising her bed linen shield even higher.

"And why not?"

"She's gone," Mrs. Bodkins blurted out.

"Well, where did she go?" Justin asked reasonably. He suddenly looked suspicious. "What scrape is she in now?"

"Oh, I would na' call it a scrape, my Lord," Mrs. Bodkins said conscientiously. "Leastways, I don't consider it one."

"Well, if she is out upon the estate, tell me and I'll meet her. I could use a ride."

Mrs. Bodkins' courage failed her at this. She stood mutely, staring at him with helpless eyes.

"Mrs. Bodkins," Justin said gently, "if she is out doctoring again, I promise I won't be angry. Oh my God! She's not delivering Mrs. Timble's baby, is she?"

"No, my Lord. Dr. James did that. It was a fine, strapping laddie—seven and one half pounds he is,

183

with the merriest blue eyes," Mrs. Bodkins chattered, eager to change the subject.

Justin regarded her with a vulture's eye. Mrs. Bodkins, dismally accepting there was no escape, picked up her swooning courage and gave it a sturdy shake. She squared her shoulders and looked Justin resolutely in the eye. "She's gone-gone, Master Justin. She's left for good."

"Left for good?" Justin repeated blankly. "But why?" Suddenly he was angry, fully knowing the answer, but refusing to believe Meg would leave him—his employ, that is.

"I think ye're the only one that kens that, my Lord. 'Tis certain I don't know, she would'na say a word. But ye made the wee colleen cry, Master Justin."

"Oh my God!" Justin exclaimed, exasperation masking his deeper feelings. "Where did she go?"

"I don't know," Mrs. Bodkins confessed, rather weakly this time.

"You don't know! Don't gammon me, Mrs. Bodkins, you must know. You couldn't have let her depart without knowing where she was going—whether she was safe!" Coming from any other man than the Earl, Justin's demand could easily have been mistaken for a plea.

"No, I don know," Mrs. Bodkins retorted stoutly. But she felt obliged to add, "But if I did know, I would'na tell it, for I promised her I would'na say a word. And that I won't, Master Justin. You leave the poor lass alone," she admonished firmly, steeling herelf against his displeasure.

Justin, realizing that the determined Mrs. Bodkins would not likely aid him, turned smartly on his heel and stalked off. "Wh—where are ye going, Master Justin?"

"To get another bottle," Justin threw over his

shoulder. "I say good riddance to the chit. She would have been the death of me if she had stayed!"

"If she isn't already," Mrs. Bodkins murmured, shaking her head at the retreating male form. Holding her linens close for comfort, she sighed over the sad fate which had befallen the great House of Argyle.

Chapter Twelve

Hunting Meggie

"Cor, here comes his nibs again!" shrilled Naughty Lizzy in excitement, jabbing a red satin elbow into Buxom Molly's padded side.

"Blimey, so it is, and back so soon!" Molly exclaimed, her eyes taking on a bright glow beneath her paint.

"Who is he?" whispered Little Nell, the youngest and newest inhabitant of the Three Pillars, an establishment whose name proudly dated back to the fact that it was the third edifice ever constructed in the humble village of Argyle, the church and the smithy being the first.

As the newest, Nell was the only one who still earned her wage solely as a barmaid. Her eyes widened as they followed the tall, elegantly dressed man who wended his way through the rowdy crowd. His walk was dignified, only the knowledgeable guessing he was well to live.

"That, ducky, is the Earl of Argyle," Naughty Lizzy informed Little Nell proudly. "And let me tell yer, he's noble in every way, ken what I mean?"

"Business is sure a pleasure with him," Molly sighed gustily. "Makes yer feel a squeeze for taking his blunt."

"Yeh, I feel like I oughta' be payin' him," Naughty Lizzy agreed.

"Does he come here often?" Little Nell asked, unable to take her eyes away from the compelling stranger.

"He does now," grunted Lizzy. "Used to be he'd never step his foot in here, too proper and good for that. Me sister's in service in London town for a nob and she said he'd be of same name there."

"Yeah, he's getting a different name now!" Molly interjected. "Though it queers me how. Some hoity toity people around here been calling him the "Wicked Earl." If that don't beat all! He ain't ever been wicked to me. Leastways, not in no ways I don't like."

"Some tart up and diddled him," Lizzy continued sharply. "You know, one of those coldhearted, priggish morts that's too good to give a man some comfort on a cold night. So he comes here, swilling blue ruin like water. Gawd!" she said suddenly. "Think what he'd be like without the stuff!"

"Cor," Molly exclaimed. "'Tain't fair, he drinking hisself to death over that no-good trollop! If only I was her, I'd treat him right." Molly's chest was overswelling its restraints in indignation.

"You know her?" Little Nell breathed.

"I only know her name—Meg," Molly whispered confidingly. "He's mum as an oyster about her. But sometimes he'll call you that so tender-like when he forgets. It fair breaks your heart, it does."

"That Meg's a damn fool," spat Liz. "To have a man like that, hot for hers! He ain't the usual sort, and I've seen plenty of them."

"Say, Little Nell," Molly said warmly, "here's your chance. If you're ever going to start the business, I'd

187

go try it with his nibs over there. Best first a girl could ever want!"

"Best second or third a girl could ever want," Naughty Liz added. "Molly, you softhearted jade, giving him to her. But I'll go along with yer. Honey," she said maternally to Nell, who was blushing hotly and halfheartedly shaking her head, "go on, he'll treat yer proper-like. Let him call you Meggy and be sweet to him, you hear?"

"Yeah, the poor cove oughta have a little kindness," said the tender Molly, sighing sadly for the Earl.

The door to Justin's room cracked open quietly. A nattily attired figure slid in, closing the door soundlessly.

Within the stygian room, a solitary man sat slouched in a chair, unpolished Hessians rudely set upon the nearby table. The boots threatened to topple the brandy bottle that stood perilously close to them. If that one fell, a domino effect would occur, surrounded as it was by myriad other bottles of various quantities and kinds.

The dapper figure blinked, and blinked again. "Justin?" it whispered hesitantly into the darkness. The sound echoed back.

"Ahh, Edward," a lazy voice returned. Justin was deep in his cups, tap-hacket to be exact.

Now the two types of men that drink are the very weak and the very strong. The weak man because he can't gainsay perdition and the strong man because he pursues perdition. Justin was pursuing perdition religiously.

He took another drink, not turning his head. "Ah, Edward," he repeated.

"Justin? Wasn't sure it was you, old man." Edward

spoke cheerfully, now that he was certain he spoke to his very own kith and kin. "Must be the new fashion you are sporting."

"Uhuh."

A silence ensued in which Justin appeared sunk in his own thoughts. Finally, he rolled his head toward Edward. "Where have you been?"

"Oh, visiting at Ferdie's. A great entertainer, Ferdie. Has prime cattle."

"S'thought you were in school," Justin slurred on a growl.

"No, no. Don't go back 'till this coming week. That's what I'd like to discuss with you. I've hatched a brilliant scheme, you see. The quarter is quite into itself. I'll be devilish hard-set to catch up. Ain't as well set up in the bone box as you, you know. Must have gotten Mother's wits there. Unfortunate," he apologized, "but there you have it."

Justin snorted. What a hum. Edward was as sharp as a tack. Did he think he could bamboozle his own brother?

Edward continued quickly, fearing he had laid it on much too thick and rare. "So the best thing would be for me to sit this one out. It'd give me a span to mature, become responsible and all. And only consider, Dean Hoffer might be so grateful to you that he'd name a hall after you, what?"

Justin merely raised one drunk eyebrow. "Sssit down. Have a glass with me," he offered, waving his unsteady one toward the direction of his boots. "'S'got to be one there somewhere."

Actually, there were several scattered amongst the bottles like wildflowers in a field. Edward eased himself into the chair and surveyed the grimy, reeking array before him. Spying a likely candidate, quite sticky but uncompromisingly empty, he lifted it gingerly and

189

stumbled across the room to the bed, unexpected articles of clothing catching at his feet. He snatched a crumpled cravat that lay there and proudly returned it to his chair so that he could polish the glass in leisure. Justin followed his movements fuzzily.

"Been thinking on your prop-propa—plan. Good idea—sit this one out. But don't think you've hoaxed me. I'm no ffflat. Expect you to keep your ppromise. No larks . . . no shshams. If there are—I'll cut your lizard out."

"Right ho! That's the barber!" Edward agreed readily. "I'll be good—see if I let you cut a lizard out of me!"

His own goal achieved, Edward now studied his brother in concern. Well-satisfied with Justin's pledge, he set himself to unravel the imbroglio it appeared his normally responsible brother was evidently entangled in. It would never do, the scion of the family turning into a sot. Surely Uncle Josepheth was enough for any one family?

"Tell me, brother," Edward said conversationally, "what has transpired of late? Gads, someone should have been kind enough to put the funeral colours out in warning that the house is in blacks. I was never more shocked when I visited Mother. She was savaging her needlepoint as if it was possessed. Certainly it's a horticultural nightmare, but I don't think it in that realm—definitely no spirit to it!"

Justin hiccupped at this artistic critique.

"Quite right," Edward agreed. "I stray. But I'm clear betwattled, old man. Been hearing such strange ondits. Most queer one is that you've given Malissa her cogne'."

"Have. Last time I was in London." Justin nodded up and down.

"Whatever for?"

Justin considered for a moment, maybe two. Then he looked at the perpetrator of such furious thought and scowled. "Grew tired of her."

"'Pon rep!" exclaimed Edward. This was indeed plain speaking without the bark, something unforeseen from his diplomatic brother. He asked in dread, "You never said that to her, old boy? She must have kicked up a devil of a dust!"

"No—no." Justin lied. It hurt his head even to remember Malissa's vitriolic comments. "Gave her a set of matched bays and carriage, parted am . . . icably," he explained, shamelessly disregarding the truth.

"Oh, then all's settled on that head. Perhaps you can clarify another matter?"

"Shooooot!" Justin cried enthusiastically, pointing one cocked finger at his head in zealous mime, making Edward unaccountably nervous.

"Ah . . . well . . . yes. Regret to tell you this, but saw Mrs. Bodkins next. She fell upon my neck crying."

"Teetotalling busybody," Justin said in explanation.

"Yes, but that don't give her the right to turn watering pot on my new coat. She's positively vaporish. Seems you drank the cellar dry, old fellow."

"I have?" Justin asked, displaying more feelings than he had so far. "Need to order some more," he said in consternation.

"That puts paid to that," Edward observed dryly as Justin lifted his glass. "Well, now for the last trifle. Mrs. Bodkins blubbered into my cravat some twaddle about you frequenting the bawdy h—" Edward halted as two malevolent, bloodshot eyes affixed themselves on him. "I see. Well, 'tis no bread and butter of mine, but it seems your present deportment is earning you a reputation, Justin. Not to wrap it up in clean linen, old boy, they say you'll soon surpass Uncle Josepheth on that score and he's been at it a far sight longer

191

than you."

"'S'true," Justin hiccupped glumly, but added fiercely, "but I don't touch servants!"

"Very commendable. One must draw the line somewhere. And pray, forgive me, my remarkably slow wits, you know, but why this, what shall we say— heigh-ho, might as well say it with no roundaboutations—why this raking?"

Justin remained silent, twisting his glass and peering into its golden contents as if it held all the answers. He sighed. "Meg's bolted," he murmured quietly.

Now this statement would appear to be a non sequitur of no small standing. However, to his brother, it was an enlightening statement. After a moment, Edward sucked in his breath and asked, "Why?"

"I kissed her."

"You kissed her! Was that all?" Edward asked in bewilderment.

"No, kissed her thoroughly," Justin admitted sadly. He hiccupped disconsolately.

"No, buck up old man, that can't have signified," Edward objected. "Meggy's not the sort to take snuff over such a trifle. I mean, stands to reason, she kissed that rum touch Pavnor once." Justin snarled at him. "She certainly wouldn't cavail at you."

"She did." Justin despondently sipped his drink.

"Must be losing your address, brother. Was it all that bad?"

"No, enjoyed it," Justin said firmly.

"Then it couldn't be the kiss," Edward reasoned frowning, "What did you say to her? You said something to her before you kissed her, didn't you?"

"'Did. Told her I didn't like her ffiancé. Told her she'd be better off as a mistressss than his wife."

"What?" Edward yelped, his fingers almost ungluing from his sticky glass. "Never say you offered Meg a

192

carte blanche?"

"No, dash it! Why does everybody ask that? She asked me that—me! Told her—wouldn't have her ash mistress . . . don't engage in affairsh with lower orders . . . you know that!"

"Well, Justin, you certainly didn't hide your teeth behind your hand," Edward said, growing irritated. "What did Meg say to that?"

Justin smiled. His bloodshot eyes took on an approving warmth. "Sssent me to the rightabouts. Told me she had her prin . . . ciples, too. Told me she didn't have affairsh with arristo . . . cratic prigs like me! Ha! Told me that! So I kissed her!"

"Poor Meg," Edward said, now very displeased with his dear brother. "No wonder she took French leave."

Justin peered at Edward, first in astonishment, and then in puzzlement. Edward understood something that remained elusive to him. He had tried all these hellish weeks to understand it and here Edward appeared to comprehend it in a day.

Edward looked at his brother severely. "Well, Justin, you've made a fine hash of it. 'Twasn't right to serve Meg such Turkish treatment. But that's water under the bridge. First things first! Got to dry you out. You've wallowed in self-pity much too long, not to mention certain ladybirds' arms. It's not like you to be cowardly."

"Ain't a coward," objected Justin. "Never been called one. Ought to call you out!"

"Justin, don't be a dullard. You can't call your own brother out—bad ton, dear boy, very bad ton. As I was saying—"

"You were?"

"Yes. Next, you come down from your high ropes and go find the girl and tell her you love her. You two can make plans from there. Though it might have to be marriage if Meggy is as handy with the poker as you say

193

she is."

"She's damned good with a skillet, too," Justin said, brightening.

"That settles it. Must do the honorable thing and marry her."

Justin stared at Edward, thunderstruck. "You said I love her?"

"You love her," affirmed Edward, as if reassuring a child.

"Do you think I could marry her?" Justin asked in excitement.

"Don't see why not," Edward considered. "It's unfortunate that she's a maid, born on the wrong side of the blanket as well. But better to suffer ostracism for that than because you're a loose screw. Got to stop terrifying the villagers, what? You've plenty estates to retire to together. If that don't serve, you can travel abroad. Family won't disown you. I mean, stands to reason, never disowned Uncle all these years. And you're the head of the family—who'll gainsay you? Certainly won't be mother. Unless you don't let her have Meg for petit point."

"The ffiancé went with her," Justin said suddenly and grimly. "She might be married already."

"Oh."

"No. She'll marry me if I have to make her a widow."

Justin sat a moment in deep meditation. Suddenly, his lips twitched. He looked at Edward warmly. Brother understood brother. "Thank you."

"Think nothing of it," Edward offered gruffly.

Justin pulled his feet from the table and leaned over to set his glass down, unerringly upon another. He then reached his hand out to Edward. The two men clasped hands and shook strongly.

*   *   *

Three weeks later, Mr. Tothwell looked up calmly from an intriguing document that he had been analytically, and therefore enjoyably, perusing. Mr. Twitterhold, his gangly, ferret-faced secretary, had entered precipitously, his small eyes darting back and forth, his large nose twitching.

Mr. Tothwell sighed. Mr. Twitterhold performed his offices faultlessly. It was a mere misfortunte that he forever resembled a startled rodent. "Yes, Mr. Twitterhold?" he inquired, not the slightest hint of irritation ruffling his composed voice.

"Sir! There is a gentleman outside who desires an interview with you. I tried to explain that you were occupied, but he would not be refused. His name is—"

"His name is Justin, Lord Devenish, the seventh Earl of Argyle," a deep voice graciously supplied from behind. Mr. Twitterhold squeaked and twitched nervously.

Mr. Tothwell adjusted his monocle slightly. A tall, commanding figure with an admirable point-de-vice appearance stood at ease in the doorway.

"Evidently," Mr. Tothwell observed after quietly surveying him. He glanced at his secretary, whose mouth now twitched in harmony with his nose. "That will be all, Mr. Twitterhold." Mr. Twitterhold jumped and attempted speech; thinking better of it, however, he scurried from the room. "Do come in, my Lord, and be seated. Please allow me to present myself. I am Mr. Tothwell."

"Evidently," the Earl observed with a smile.

"I am honored to meet you, my Lord. Now, how may I be of assistance?" His myopic eyes displayed nought but the mildest of curiosity.

"I have been informed that through your respected firm, my staff acquired a housemaid by the name of Meggy Smith. She has since then left our employ. I am

195

desirous of locating her and thought you might be of service in that regard," Justin explained politely. He sat relaxed within the brown chair, elbows gently resting on the chair wings, his hands forming an isosceles triangle. His cool grey eyes regarded the little man before him with serene assessment.

"I see, my Lord," Mr. Tothwell responded. "And may I be so bold as to inquire why you are desirous of locating this person? It is to be sincerely hoped that she did not abscond with any family possessions."

"'Deed no, nothing so monumental as all that. 'Tis a mere trifle. She left without rightly claiming her last wages, and I merely wish to send them to her."

"How generous, my Lord," Mr. Tothwell said appreciatively. "It is uncommon civil for a man of your exalted stature to bestow such considered interest in your serving staff."

"No more uncommon that a man of your illustrious firm condescending to act as referring agent for a maid to that staff."

A silence settled upon the room. Two masters of reserve studied each other with apparent leisure. Mr. Tothwell's eyes soon held a shade of pleasure, though even the closest of observers might have been reasonably forgiven for failing to remark it. "There is nothing irregular in that, I assure you. I was merely performing a service for a valued client."

"Ah yes, you speak of the lady she resided with before her services, no doubt?"

"Yes, that could very well be," Mr. Tothwell agreed, with the slightest of smiles.

"Thank you. And could you be so obliging as to supply me with her name?" Justin asked with casual interest.

"I regret that it is not within my power to do so. That information is most confidential."

"Perhaps you can inform me of Meggy Smith's new address."

"I am sorry, my Lord, I do not know it," Mr. Tothwell, returned, quite unperturbed.

"Ah, but I think you do," Justin disagreed amiably. "I noted that you had no need of recourse to your files when the subject of Meggy Smith was introduced, or even now, when I asked her whereabouts. This leads me to believe that you do indeed hold knowledge of her present employ."

Mr. Tothwell blinked once, and solely once. His expression of polite interest altered not one whit. The solicitor was developing a fondness for this contained man, if man was indeed what you could call him. "You are very observant, my Lord. And, in truth, you are correct. However, that information is also confidential."

With surprising speed, the cool Earl uncoiled from his relaxed position. In an instant, he possessed a comprehensive stranglehold upon Mr. Tothwell, who dangled ignobly over his very own desk. The solicitor was aware of a distant cracking, as if a small glass had been broken.

"I fully understand the importance of confidentiality to your clients," Justin said. "It is to be applauded. And allow me to assure you that such information will be held in the strictest of confidences, once you are obliging enough to impart it to me."

Mr. Tothwell strove for dignity. He found it excessively difficult with the blood rushing so alarmngly to his head. His eyes bulged under their own direction. "I will not tell you, my Lord," he managed to whisper through harassed vocal cords.

"I believe it would be advisable for you to do so."

"I do believe it would," Mr. Tothwell's precision forced him to admit. "Unhappily, I will not. My

197

directions were clear!"

Justin studied his victim for one discerning moment. He then lowered the pale solicitor so that his feet touched solid floor once again. As he straightened Mr. Tothwell's mangled cravat, he discovered it to be spotted with red; flexing his hand, he found it cut. He studied Mr. Tothwell carefully to find his monocle shattered, but gamely hanging to its ribbon.

"Sorry, old man, do accept my apologies," Justin offered as Mr. Tothwell raised the battered item for inspection. "Another one will be sent to you directly. Your loyalty to Meggy is regrettable, but I cannot help but understand such devotion. If, perchance, you have the honor of seeing Miss Smith again, be pleased to inform her that she may expect a visit from me in the near future, for despite your inconvenient faithfulness, I will find her." And with a courteous bow and pleasant nod, he strode from the office.

Mr. Tothwell allowed himself a bemused smile. He said gently to the closed door, "Yes, I fear you are right, my Lord, I fear you are right. Though I do feel you will be presented with a surprise if you ever meet 'Meggy' again."

He shook himself from his concentration, and sat down. Raising the legal document he had been studying close to his face, he began to read.

Lady Linton hesitantly sipped her hot tea. She was dressed in a charming morning dress of rose silk, and though her figure was elegant, it was slighter even than that which was considered "fashionably slim."

Lady Linton had been on the town for little over a fortnight. Scaling the social heights nimbly, she had captured the fickle hearts of the haut ton. She was an original, and decidedly all the crack. Well-known

198

fortune hunters, mooning halflings, and nonpareils all fell at her slippered feet. For all this excess of favor, however, Lady Linton had earned the soubriquet of "The Elusive." No schoolroom miss, she competently maneuvered flirts and amorous cads. No man was left in doubt that her candid, witty heart remained unerringly unobtainable.

Lady Linton would have been mortified to hear the gossips discuss the intriguing sadness that would suddenly invade her lovely blue eyes. Matrons would knowingly shake their heads, decreeing that it must come from the loss of her dear grandfather. Young debutantes would sigh over that faraway look, certain it came from an unrequited passion. As for Megan, she never suspected that she displayed anything but unadulterated involvement within the local whirl. Self-preservation demanded that she believe that she was forgetting "Him," for surely there must be a least an hour—of total moments combined—that she did not think of the Earl.

She looked up with a delighted smile for the prim little man that sat on the settee opposite her. "And what brings you to the hub of society, Mr. Tothwell? I see that you are looking exceedingly well. Is that not a new glass that you sport? It looks to be gold."

"Yes, indeed it is, my Lady. It was a present from a gentleman. I see that you are also looking well, though you appear thinner than I remember."

Megan gave a trill of laughter. "It is a small wonder with all my reckless gadding about. The whirl of London life keeps me fashionably slim. It is not marvelous if I am burnt to the socket."

Mr. Tothwell sipped his tea, leaving the noncommittal pause to speak for him. "Madame," he then said, 'I deemed it my duty to post to London to inform you of a visit I received on your behalf."

199

"How intriguing. I do hope it was not some disagreeable creditor. Never say that I have outrun the constable?" Megan said, lightly quizzing.

"No, Madame, you are quite within your means. Even if you were not, I would never have any difficulties in dealing with such a person," he gently reminded her, with neither conceit nor pride. It was merely fact. "This visitor was a gentleman of your past acquaintance."

Mr. Tothwell raised his new glass to his considering orb to study the effects of this announcement. Lady Linton set her china cup upon its saucer and shakily pushed it onto the service tray. The solicitor noted that the Lady turned precisely one shade lighter.

Megan's words were quite airy, however. "This is even more curious. I do hope you mean to inform me of who it is, for I can't imagine who it might be. I was never one for guessing games."

"Certainly, Madame—that is the purpose of my sojourn to London. My visitor was your late employer, the Seventh Earl of Argyle."

"The devil!"

"No, Madame, though his demeanor and wit might suggest to me that he is none other."

"Dear me, from that I gather he gave you an umpleasant turn."

Mr. Tothwell seemed almost to smile at this. "No, not exactly. I admit I was surprised to find I rather enjoyed the interview."

"Well, if you could, I am glad of it," Megan said with some asperity. She did not wish for Mr. Tothwell to have loathed Justin's visit, but that the unflappable solicitor should enjoy a chat with the object of her disfavor roused her ire. "And what did that—ah, the Earl, want?"

"Why, to ascertain your present location."

"What?"

"Yes. He professed that he still owed you back pay," Mr. Tothwell explained blandly.

"He owes me nothing! He is a conniving arrogant, past—busybody! I hope you put a flea in his ear and sent him about his business."

"No, Madame, I merely informed him that your present direction was confidential information which I could not let out." Tothwell could never imagine a man of his stamp and character being so ragmannered as to put a flea in another man's ear.

"Ho! Mr. Tothwell, you are a trump!" Megan's eyes sparkled with unsurpressed glee. "And what did he say to that?"

"Well, he didn't actually say anything," Mr. Tothwell reported with an irritating regard for the facts. Megan's face fell in bewilderment.

"He said nothing? He simply left it at that?"

"No, not a word, Madame, for you see, he then proceeded to strangle me. That is when he strongly advised me to divulge your present whereabouts."

"Good gracious God, the monster! Faith, he hasn't even gone that far with me, and we were always coming to cuffs."

"Ah—yes, indeed," Mr. Tothwell murmured, once again feeling the slackening of calm, a disheartening condition only experienced in the presence of Lady Linton. "He quite destroyed my shirt and literally crushed my glass—but he replaced it with this one. Highly decent of him, I'd say."

"Lud, it's the least he could do for such reprehensible behavior. I deeply regret that you suffered such an unpleasant scene, though I'd give a monkey to know why Justin cut up so stiff."

"Oh no, my Lady, he was quite cordial through the whole affair. He did not once raise his voice in anger."

201

Megan's eyes widened, and then she giggled, and the giggle turned into an infectious, hearty laugh. "Oh," she said as she wiped tears from her eyes, "I can very well believe it. It would be just like Justin when upon his dignity."

"So I thought, Madam." Mr. Tothwell felt proud his reading of character was correct. "Though it pains me to say that my sources testify otherwise. It appears that his Lordship has not acted so coolly previously. To be frank, he has been leading a life as such that must give rise to talk. Indeed, my contacts were so firm as to inform me that he has become the scourge of his village within a matter of three or four short weeks. They have titled him the "Wicked Earl," a highly precipitous and severe title in my estimation."

"What?" exclaimed Megan. "Impossible! Justin is the highest stickler, never one to go beyond the line of propriety." Suddenly, she blushed. "Well, generally he does not."

"Madame, I do not mean to disagree, but my sources are the most reliable and creditable, and they beg to differ. It was reported that he has maintained a steady stupor, gambled, raced, and frequented certain— houses."

"He's taken up with haymarket ware?" Megan practically shouted in disbelief.

Mr. Tothwell thanked the absent Earl for the new gold glass, which, due to its superior fit, tended to remain in one's orb, even under the most stressing of circumstances. "Ah, yes, Madame, it would appear so," he confirmed with a cough.

"Why, the cad!" Megan bounded from the chair to pace across the room in a more energetic than mannerly fashion. "He merrily enters into happy debauchery and succeeds in becoming the scourge of his village within a wondrously short time. The 'Wicked Earl,' indeed!

202

Infamous! While I, mind you, claim the title of 'The Elusive!' Does that not beat all!" Megan stopped on a sputter. She gulped back her next vitriolic comment, her jaw mutinously jutting out. "And he swore he did not have affairs with the lower orders," she ground out indignantly.

Regardless of its superior fit, the gold glass fell from Mr. Tothwell's eye. Megan, cathing his reddened expression on an overly enthusiastic turn in her revolutions about the parlor, stopped short. She sucked in her breath with resolution. "I fear my anger leads me into unseemly behavior. Pray, forgive me—it is my regrettable temper." She hastened to her chair and sat down gracefully, a volcano come to rest.

She smiled quite brightly. "So, Justin is fit and enjoying himself?"

"I would not describe him as fit, my Lady." Her companion considered his words as he located and replaced his glass. "There is no doubt of his elegant dress and bearing, but he is unquestionably thin, and I noted he appeared rather pale. Indeed, one might even say haggard. Evidently his excessive habits have not proved salubrious."

"But then, why did he do it?" Megan couldn't help asking in bewidlerment, and just a little hurt. Anger, though, was close behind. How dare he endanger his health!

"Perhaps, my Lady, for the same reason you fled to London and stormed the haut ton like a dervish. He has become the byword of his village—you have become the toast of the town. And though running the risk of being considered presumptuous, I must observe that you, also, my Lady, are unquestionably thin." Megan's eyes flew to his in consternation and she flushed.

Of a sudden, that very prim, businesslike, balding

little man took on the guise of a gentle father. "Precisely," he said with a small nod, as Megan registered her understanding. She remained stunned. "Well, Madame, I must be leaving, though I felt it my duty to inform you of Lord Devenish's visit and subsequent interview." Arising, he bowed and crossed to the door.

"Th—thank you, Mr. Tothwell," Megan stammered in severe agitation.

Mr. Tothwell felt well-satisfied, for deep in his solicitor's heart he knew that if Megan had employed a glass, she would have easily lost it. With his hand on the doorknob, he halted to add, "Indeed! How remise of me—I forgot. His Lordship requested me to deliver a message. He desired me to inform you that despite the setbacks, he intends to find you. Perhaps, Madame, for the sake of his immortal soul—and only for that, of course—you could allow him to catch you this time?"

With that, he bowed and exited.

Chapter Thirteen

Justin Has The Pleasure Of
Meeting Lady Linton

Lady Linton's friends and admirers soon began to fear for her sanity, for that most confident of ladies had taken to nervous fits and starts. She attended all the elite functions and flirted and danced, yet her famous faraway look had turned into a harried searching of the rooms. Deep voices from behind made her positively skittish. In fact, as one of her favorites had discovered, Lady Linton had developed the habit of keeping her back to the wall.

The young girls sighed, sure she went in dread of some villainous tormentor. The older but wiser knew better, and they shook their heads in regret that one so young should fall prey to imaginary persecution. Hadn't her late grandfather been eccentric?

Just like a foretold tooth extraction, however, the fateful night arrived. It transpired without warning the night of the Suffolk Ball. Megan, busily employed in fending off the lovelorn Sir Roderick, the youngest of her court, failed even to hear the voice of Nemesis.

Indeed, it could have been a bellow for all it mattered and she still would have mistaken it, so intent in stemming Sir Roderick's passionate rhetoric was she.

Now Sir Roderick was not that wicked a youth, merely overly infatuated and excessively verbal on that head. Sir Roderick's poetic spirit had divined that tonight was the night of all nights to inform his goddess that she was the sun to his earth, the stars to his night, and the shore to his ocean. In other words, he was besotted and would not rest until she was his very own.

A more experienced man might have tumbled that no matter his mystic intuition, no night would be the night to claim his beloved if he was clunch enough to do so upon a crowded dance floor, and in a rousing country dance at that. Alas, Sir Roderick did not possess such plebeian common sense, a mere crush unable to deter his dying devotion. He proceeded with the finest declamatory fashion to dump the butter boat, leaving Megan to thinly smile at her swain while her mind desperately sought an escape before she drowned in the syrup of Sir Roderick's poetic fancy.

Thus so nobly employed, Megan failed to catch the united gasp emitted upon the entrance of three gentlemen. The immediate orchestra of chatter muffled Lord Suffolk's elderly butler's rasped announcement The seventh Earl of Argyle, his younger brother and heir apparent, and the Earl's friend, Standon, the Duke of Andover, had arrived.

The fashionably bored voices spewed out the on-dits of Justin's infamous behavior as fast as their ennui permitted. Justin, accustomed to creating a stir upon his entry, did not heed it. He had not exaggerated when he told Megan that he was one of the finest catches of the season and thus the cynosure of the public eye.

"Well, old man, I'll leave you to do the pretty." Edward said cheerily, and clapped Justin on the back

"You'll see that I'm right. Best thing to do is to come to London for a spell, enjoy the diversions, what?" With this, Edward left, definitely listing toward the card room. Justin grimaced, but allowed his departure.

"And what was that all about?" queried Standon in amusement.

"Nothing." Justin's cool grey eyes smiled to his friend. "I was merely blue-deviled and Edward, ever the young opportunist, persuaded me that a bolt to London would do the trick—and naturally I should bring him along."

"Of course," Standon grinned in return. He and Justin were fast friends. His perceptive green eyes did not once display his concern for the changes wrought in Justin. Justin had said nothing. Standon would ask nothing.

"Then certainly, let us repair for refreshment and fortification," he suggested. As the two men stood together in conversation, they heard a young reedy voice call out urgently, "Make way! Make way!"

A very intense young man pushed by them, holding two sloshing glasses before him. His air was that of Ganymede carrying ambrosia to Mount Olympus and nothing less.

Yes, Megan had sent her besotted Galahad for refreshment. She had cherished an idea of escape, but, short of vaulting over chairs and cuffing her encircling court, she was sadly trapped.

"And why is Sir Roderick in such a mad dash?" queried Justin with true amusement.

"Why, he carries lemonade to his new goddess, my dear man," Standon said with mock seriousness. Sir Roderick's romantic flights were not hidden from the ton's delighted eye. Indeed, they counted upon him to liven up a flat affair with his public proposals and declarations. "But this time, she truly is a goddess."

207

"Oh?" Justin inquired without interest. He and Standon slowly followed in Sir Roderick's weaving, human-defying path.

"Without a doubt," Standon assured him. "She has the beauty and mischievousness of Aphrodite, but the swiftness for escape of Artemis. They call her 'The Elusive.'"

"Her defenses still hold, then?"

"A veritable fortress, my dear Justin, albeit a charming and wealthy one."

"Do I detect an interest in that direction?" Justin quizzed his friend.

"Lord no, the Lady is the sort to catch at your heart and lead you a merry dance down the aisle," Standon said amiably. "And my roving days are not yet ended, though many a man would be happy to do just that for her." Unconsciously, he and Justin continued with Sir Roderick on his pilgrimage to his worshipped being.

Justin froze when he spied the young man's goddess, for that particular deity had once dusted his study. There Meggy stood, the woman that blessed his nights in dreams and tormented his days in memories. She wore the finest of silks in the latest of modes, but Justin had little difficulty recognizing his erstwhile maid. "What the devil—who is that?"

"Why, 'The Elusive'—Megan Linton, Viscountess of Marchington," Standon replied, puzzled at Justin's vehement reacion.

"Countess!" exclaimed Justin. Suddenly he heard Megan's throaty laugh and musical voice—totally devoid of the country brogue and delivered in the finest of well-bred accents. He growled and strode forward.

"Justin!" protested a startled Standon, following in his wake.

The aristocratic sea parted swiftly for the two men, one in a towering rage and one in a surprised fluster.

Justin stepped up to the "The Elusive" and tapped her strongly on her shoulder.

Megan turned with a welcoming smile upon her lips, desperately hoping that someone had come to rescue her from Sir Roderick. Her smile froze as she surveyed Justin. He definitely was not the rescuer she desired. One look into his smouldering eyes and Megan's glass slipped through nerveless fingers. It fell unnoticed and unmourned by both. Surrounding bystanders were not as indifferent, however, for it was upon them the contents splashed and dashed.

Standon soon pulled up, a breathless second to Justin. With a desperate effort to camouflage his friend's freakish behavior, not to mention the daft actions of "The Elusive," he gracefully stepped forward, resolutely ignoring the crunch of glass beneath his feet, and offered with aplomb, "My dear Lady Linton, do allow me to present my closest of friends, the Earl of Devenish."

He frowned severely as neither took up his brilliant lead, both merely staring at each other like hostile statues. The surrounding people, finally looking above a paltry glass and staining drink, began to find the couple before them of more moment.

"He desires to dance with you," Standon said with force and pushed Justin toward Megan.

"Yes, my Lady, I do," Justin threatened, finally regaining his voice.

He grasped Megan's trembling hand and dragged her to the floor. The band, with superb perversity, struck up a waltz. He grasped her and swung her into the dance. "My God, what are you doing here, you little fool?"

"What do you think? I'm dancing," Megan retorted disagreeably, for her knees shook and only Justin's harsh hold kept her from crumbling into a heap upon the polished floor.

"And why, pray tell, is my runaway maid dancing at the Suffolk Ball?" Justin asked, choosing to be cuttingly sarcastic.

"I'm Cinderella?" Megan asked tartly.

"Cinderella parading as the Viscountess of Marchington, the heiress? What a strange and unusual turn to that good tale, for I swear it never read that way."

"Parading as? No such thing!" Megan sputtered ineffectually, her frazzled nerves taking refuge in fury.

"Yes, parading as! Does your mistress know that you impersonate her? She is your mistress?"

"I have no mistress!"

"My God! Never say you walked in here as bold as brass and impersonated a lady you do not even know!"

"Justin, do cut line." She pinned a belated smile to her face as she saw others look toward them. "Pray, do not be such a chucklehead or I swear I'll cuff you right here and now and send all the old tabbies into swooning."

"Perhaps a slap would suffice? It proved sufficient last time."

Megan quickly looked down, lidding her hurt. A frigid pause ensued. Growling, Justin unconsciously held Megan closer, fully aware of his ungentlemanly behavior, but unable to stop himself. It felt right to hold Meggy near again, and he damned her for it.

"Don't hold me so close," Megan hissed, flusing. "It is not proper!"

"And I suppose you are?"

"Yes, as a matter of fact, I am! You over-conceited, slow-witted fop!" Megan forced the words out through a wooden smile.

"A fop! Come, Meggy, I daresay I am many things, all of which you have categorically called me since you

210

first clapped eyes on me, but a fop, my dear? I beg to differ," Justin said congenially, his broad-shouldered, slim-hipped figure a potent testimony in his defense.

"Oh, how foolish of me, do let me alter the word," Megan returned with malicious sweetness. "Perhaps rakehell would be more accurate?"

"Rakehell?" Justin considered the word. He shook his head decisively. "No indeed, Meg, that is still wide of the mark."

"Now, my Lord, why such modesty? My ears ring with the stories of the 'Wicked Earl.' Faith, I am impressed! You accomplish in mere weeks a title which others have devoted whole lifetimes in pursuing. Uncle Josepheth must feel totally cast in the shade by you."

"Touché, my dear. But nevertheless, I am who I say I am, which is more than you can boast, my charming deceiver. Perhaps you would like to tell me your schemes, hmm, little adventuress? I'm sure I'll find them quite intriguing," Justin encouraged in velvet tones.

"Now, Justin, do not mistake the situation and promptly disabuse yourself of the odious notion that you hold anything over my head," Megan warned hastily, disliking his gleaming look. "I truly am Lady Linton, so wipe that evil smirk off your face this instant."

"So you are that respected Lady, but still claim I have nothing to hold over your deceiving head? Meg— Lady Linton, as you will—if you are indeed that personage, then why were you my maid? I highly doubt that that will do you credit. Choose which you like, my dear—a lady parading as a maid, or a maid parading as a lady, both are equally reprehensible and will destroy your reputation in the telling."

"Justin, what can you be thinking? You can't

honestly be considering tattling it about—why that would be utterly, utterly villainous!"

"I just might," Justin laughed recklessly. "After all, I am the 'Wicked Earl.' And though new to the title, I can but do my poor best to uphold it. Especially when it proves to be so—enjoyable."

Megan simply stared, almost losing her step. "You are jesting!" she exclaimed after a moment.

"No, Meggy, I am not. I intend to know your game, will you, nill you. So you might as well be a good girl and tell me now." Megan bit her lip and looked positively mulish.

"Tell me!" Justin demanded, his voice cracking like a whip.

"Don't order me like that! I am no longer your servant, so do not think you can bully me!" Megan retorted pertly, fully knowing the danger yet unable to turn away. "I am your equal in rank, you know. A sad letdown, I'm sure, but there you have it. And I have no intentions of discussing my situation with you. Not now. Not ever!"

"By God, you will discuss it with me if you know what's good for you! If you are Lady Linton, you have grossly deceived me and my household and I demand an explanation."

"Demand all you wish! You will not get one!"

"Meggy, this is enough! Tell me what you are about, you designing minx!" He pulled her closer, glaring into her upturned face.

"Justin," Megan hissed once again, "let me go. You are attracting attention."

"Something you can ill afford in your untenable position. Right, my dear?"

"Untenable position? Stuff and nonsense! I am eminently secure—you are the one in a shaky position.

You brute it about that I was your maid and I will deny it wholeheartedly. People will either disbelieve the tale or they will say you tell it with only the illest of intentions. You, my Lord, are the one with an evil reputation, while I am respectable!"

Justin's eyes burned at this. "I don't give a damn what the world thinks about you, my high-and-mighty miss. I know you as a liar and a coward!"

Megan's eyes blurred and her hand swung up from his shoulder in reflex. Justin's warning look froze it in midair. "No, Meggy, I don't advise you to try that."

Totally frustrated and smarting from his words, Megan tried to break away from his hold. He only pulled her back to him and swung her around in the dance with added vigor. "Let me go, Justin!"

"No," he returned baldly. "You will finish out this dance with me, my girl, for you daren't make a scene."

"Oh, daren't I?" purred Megan. She promptly trod on his foot. He halted in pain and she stepped back and directed a sharp kick to his shins.

Seeing the red anger flame in Justin's eyes, Megan exclaimed and took flight, swerving through the dancing couples, many of which were coming to hasty termination in surprise. "Damn it, Meggy!" Justin bellowed. "Come back here!"

He took after her, but suffered a setback when he accidentally knocked a young debutante to the ground. She promptly fell into loud hysterics, crying that he had fiendishly ruined her new gown.

Megan sped onward, dodging and sidestepping all in her path, making a dead set for the exit doorway. As she approached it, she spied Edward, staring dazed from the center of the opening, his face registering comical disbelief. "Meg! That you?" he exclaimed as she charged at him. "What the deuce?"

213

"Edward! Can't stop! Justin after me! Stop him!" Megan panted as she rushed by.

"Yoicks! But where are you going?" he yelled after her.

"Home! Get directions later!" she threw over her shoulder.

"Right ho!" Edward agreed cheerily. "A thousand pardons, clumsy of me, old chap," Meggy heard him apologize as a heavy thud and a familier curse sounded from behind. "Here, allow me to assist you up, dear brother." Megan refused to look back, but a giggle escaped her, nevertheless. Thank God for Edward, always the most obliging of souls!

With that comforting thought, she hailed a hack, not daring to wait for her carriage, and fled into the night.

The following morning, Megan arose early in anticipation of a possible call and proceeded to throw her lady's maid into hysterics over her exact dressing. Finally satisfied with her appearance, she proceeded to the parlor, where she positioned herself upon the settee and took up her sewing, ordering Jameson, her elderly butler, to receive no one but the Earl of Argyle.

By ten, she had jabbed at her linen until it resembled one of Lady Augusta's more confused creations. Just as she jabbed at the material and pierced her thumb instead, Jameson swung wide the door and announced with impressive, resonant accents, "His Lordship, the seventh Earl of Argyle."

Justin entered and Megan pulled her thumb from her mouth like an embarrassed seven-year-old. Though his superb looks made her catch her breath, she detected a pervading weariness in him. The tired lines etched around his eyes wreaked devastation upon her sensibilities.

Justin studied Megan in return. His eyes, for some unfathomable reason, emanated a deep sadness. Where were the diabolical lights and anger of last night? Blast the man, what was he about now?

"Good morning, Justin," Megan choked out quickly, stuffing her maligned sewing to the back of the cushions.

"Good morning, my Lady," Justin returned calmly. He continued to stand, his eyes never leaving her face. Megan mentally snarled; she was at a decided disadvantage being anchored to the settee. "Won't you be seated, my Lord?"

"No, thank-you, I prefer to stand." Whereupon he paced across the room and stared out the window. An uncomfortable, interminable pause descended as both occupants covertly studied each other. Megan breathed deeply as she discovered, with melancholy, that she still loved him.

"You call me 'my Lady,' Justin. You now believe me to be the real Viscountess of Marchington? Not a scheming imposter?"

"Yes, I do. How could I think you anything but?" Justin replied in a strange voice. "After reflection, there is no other conclusion possible." He turned to Megan and leaned on the sill. "You really were an abominable maid, you know. I highly doubt there is one subservient bone in your entire body." Megan could not understand why, but suddenly she blushed.

"I thought back and it stuns me that I didn't tumble to it before this. My God, the thousands of clues! Your melodious accent, your knowledge of the ton, all your skills and breeding. Hah! And to think I asked you if you knew Megan Linton. B'Gad, that must have amused you no small amount."

"No, Justin. In truth, I was petrified out of my wits when you asked that," Megan admitted with candor.

"Now what was your reply to me? Let's see—ah yes, that Megan Linton was very much like you. Nice, neat answer, I'll give you that. Lord, what a fool I was to swallow all the farradiddles you strung me!"

"I'm dreadfully sorry about that, Justin," Megan offered contritely.

"I know you don't consider it my business—after all, I'm only the poor flat you duped—but could you be so kind as to explain why you took a position in my household? Was it a lark? How you must have delighted in my skitterwitted mother, my scamp of a brother, and, finally, me, who drank and fenced and cried out my woes upon your shoulder, you, a lowly maid, and me, the gullible, hot-tempered lord of it all!"

"No!" Megan cried out in hot denial.

"They why?"

"Because I had to!" Megan retorted, clutching her trembling hands in her lap. "You know my grandfather was considered eccentric. Perhaps, in his own way, the old dear was. But he loved me and never wanted anything but the best for me. You see, he did not leave his fortune to me without a condition. In order to obtain my inheritance, I was required to live as a maid for six months, surviving on that salary alone, or I forfeited Linton Manor and my inheritance."

"Good God!"

"You sound like Mr. Tothwell now," Megan said with a slight smile. "Grandfather wished me to understand the responsibility he left me, to understand the people that would serve me. I'll own he chose a novel way, but he accomplished just that. I understand all too well, now." She avoided Justin's searching gaze. "When I was notified of the conditions, I went to Mr. Tothwell to gain his aid in this endeavor. He is the one that discovered the position and planned my masquerade. Down to the very last detail, I assure you. Make no

216

mistake, we searched and searched for what we considered the right place, and Argyle Court appeared perfect."

"Why?"

"According to our information, it was an estate rarely frequented by its masters. Jed was sent to look after me, as an added precaution."

"Poor Meg, and then we descended upon you." Justin smiled for the first time since entering.

"Yes, as well as inviting half of London. It was too bad of you," Megan said with wry humor. "I was sure the game would be up before I started."

"Why couldn't you confide in me, Meg?" Justin said tautly, refusing to join in her amusement. His hurt was palpable. Her lies had cut deep.

"I—I couldn't tell you," Megan defended weakly.

"Why not? What did you think I'd do? Take advantage of you?"

"No, never! You must know that!" She looked at Justin and sighed. Nothing but the truth could appease this man, and she knew she would give him anything if she could but ease the pain. She stood up and forsook her settee in agitation.

"Justin, I would have told you, truly I would have. That last day, I was just steeling myself to confess, and then we had that terrible row. You were rather harsh that day, you know . . . and I was hurt . . . so I left. I no longer wished to confide in you—faith, I no longer wished to lay eyes upon you," Megan confessed with a softening smile.

"Is that the truth? My temper drove you away?" Justin queried, studying his shining Hessians.

"No, that's not the only reason," she admitted slowly.

"What was the other reason?"

Megan perused the table before her and said as

conversationally as she could, "I know you do not believe in love, that you seek a marriage of convenience. You plan to go your own way after you're married, and your wife can go her own."

"Dammit, what a fool!"

Megan did not inquire into this cryptic remark, her eyes being intently trained upon two Dresden figures, a shepherd and a shepherdess that smiled inanely at each other from across the tabletop. "I'm sure you think I stray, but I do not. And pray, do not think me puffed up in my own conceit, but when you ran through all the other heiresses on the list so scientifically and efficiently, that only left me. I—I did not want you to consider me for my fortune or my wealth. You see, I'd fallen in love with you, and though it is a very romantical notion, I—wanted you to come to—consider me for my person." Megan heard a gasp and sensed a movement, but she held her hand up in a staying manner, her eyes never straying from the Dresden figures. "I know it was sentimental, and quite idiotish, but love makes you think foolish things—like the person of your regard will naturally come to love you in return."

"Meggy, I—" Justin began.

"No, please let me finish. I did trust you, Justin, but I didn't trust myself. I couldn't take the chance of you asking Megan Linton for her hand in marriage. I was afraid I'd weaken and accept, which might only cause disaster for you and me. I could never make the comfortable wife that you desire. I find I have a terrible failing, I'm odiously jealous. I'd hate your mistresses and I know I couldn't remain in the country while you took your pleasures in town. I'm afraid I'm not very convenient." Intent on baring her faults, Megan never noticed the slow-growing rumble beneath her words.

"But, after due consideration, I see I am behaving

218

like the veriest school-room miss. 'Deed, I'm sure I could rid myself of these sentiments with . . . practice . . . perseverance . . . and if you are still in the market for a wife, perhaps we could strike a bargain . . . I mean, contract a marraige. I will strive to allow you to go your own way. You may have your mistresses, and I will—take care of myself."

"The devil you will!" Justin exploded, striding to her and rudely shaking her. Her bobbing head lost its Dresden focus and she was forced to look at him. He was thunderous.

"I will not accept that," he growled. "You will be my mistress—"

"So we are back to that—but you told me you'd not have me for a mistress," Megan objected, striving for a nonexistent composure. With her new penchant for inanimate objects, she glued her confused eyes to Justin's cravat.

"Meggy, do let me finish," Justin said with tender exasperation. "I desire you for my mistress and my wife, you enchanting idiot! I want you to marry me! And mind you, I intend to have no mistresses, and you will not have any cicisbeo, if that is what you meant by 'taking care of yourself.' I'll lock you up on bread and water before I permit that. But never fear, darling, I will endeavor to keep you sufficiently occupied so that your affections never stray. I have a confession to make as well. Despite my fine talk, I am not a very convenient person, either, though I just discovered it. Meggy," he said, taking her hands in his, "I know what I said once. I never thought I'd need or want a woman beside me for life. But I do!

"You see, I don't go on very well without you, my dear. God, you well-nigh drove me insane when you left. Looking back, I don't know what bacon-brained notion I had in my head—I suppose I thought that I

219

could marry as the world did and still have you forever by my side. Gad's, if I had managed to get a wife, she would have been terribly in the way, I'd say. But when you left, I couldn't indulge myself with those imaginings. Meg, you had become everything important to me, but I couldn't admit it. That is why I said all those cruel things that day. Convention deigned I could not take you as my wife, and honor said I could not have you as mistress. So I rejected you, and almost destroyed myself in doing so. But I came to, Meg. I realized I needed you, no matter what. That's when I started looking for you. I didn't give a tinker's damn whether you were a maid then, and if you had married that cursed groom, I intended to kill him. Meggy, I don't care now. Please believe me—I love you."

Megan's eyes flew precipitiously from Justin's cravat to his face. His eyes shone with a tender light she had never been permitted to see before. She cast him an exuberant grin and flung her arms around him with little decorum. Justin, a man of action, promptly accepted her unspoken suggestion and kissed her hungrily. He held her tighter, lovingly squeezing the air from her lungs.

Megan's head buzzed. Time stopped. She felt as if she floated in midair, which, indeed, she did, for Justin, in his exuberance, had picked her up, thus decreasing the inches between them. Neither enthralled participant took note, however, so involved in fireworks, volcanoes, and earthquakes as they were. The kiss proved totally and unsettlingly satisfying.

Justin, seeking to hold her closer, which his disordered brain did not realize was impossible, slowly set her down in order to reenvelop her. One mischievous heel caught in the back of Megan's skirt and she, much too happily engaged otherwise, was not perspicacious enough to correct the error.

Her levitated state ended. Justin, already bending over and well entwined, followed his beloved's direction. They toppled over, knocking the table and rattling the shepherd and his missus out of their bucolic peace. A sound of tearing cloth rent the air.

Justin peered down at Megan. "Meggy, that is the third coat you have ruined."

Megan grimaced. "I'm sorry, Justin."

Justin laughed. "Never fret, Meggy, I have acknowledged that I will always end up falling around you. You seem to have that singular effect upon me." He brushed her tawny hair back from her face and kissed her upon the nose. "In faith, I do believe I can grow tolerably fond of this position."

"Indeed?" murmured Megan, a twinkle in her eye and a blush upon her cheek. Justin responded by kissing her with a strong hint of why he favored that position. He then pulled back, an action Megan deemed highly unneccessary.

"Meggy . . . Megan, we can sign a contract upon which all your money remains yours. I do not wish you to ever think I married you for your fortune," Justin said gravely, resembling nothing more than a troubled schoolboy in his sincerity. Megan heaved a heavy sigh, a slight smile playing about her lips. She tugged Justin's head down and kissed him warmly.

The kiss was not short, but assuredly sweet. She was the first to pull away this time saying shakily as she traced the crow's-feet splaying from Justin's eyes, "No, my Lord, if you kiss me like that and tell me you love me every day, I will concede you are no fortune hunter."

"It will be my pleasure, my Lady."

"Besides, do think on all the pleasure we may have pending our future," Megan said lazily, a slow smile crossing her face.

"Don't smile at me like that," Justin frowned, "or I warn you, I will not be held accountable for my actions, which I assure you would be anything but proper, even for a fiancé."

"Quick, find me my poker, I must protect myself. I am a respectable girl, my Lord," Megan said, easily slipping into her country accent.

"Then I suggest we obtain a special license with all due haste," Justin advised huskily. "We'll set it for next week," he added quickly, as Megan kissed him soundly. "And then, my darling Meg, there will be no pokers. Ever!"

"Or expensive widows," she added, kissing Justin's forehead.

"Or grooms," he agreed, kissing her neck. "And you will never rudely fall asleep upon me again?"

"I never did, did I?" Megan replied, startled.

"Mm, yes you did. Night of your first mill." He kissed her cheek.

"Ohhh. Well, I am sure it was the only proper thing to do. I assure you, it will not be so the next time, upon my honor." Justin laughed. "And you, in return, won't pass out on me?" she teased.

"Trust me, fair termagant, you will never be so fortunate again. I was merely being the gentleman."

"Gentleman! Justin, you—"

"I promise you," Justin said wickedly. "Now that I have you, I intend to spend no more nights drunk— from drink, that is. I will be your lord and master once and for all!"

"Yes, my Lord," Megan said with a total lack of demureness.

"Make no mistake, Madame, I will have no mercy— you have put me through enough torment to last a lifetime. It will be just you—"

222

"And me."

"Well, and the children," he added with a suggestive grin.

"Ah, yes, those rich little Devenishes. Won't we please Lady Augusta!" With a blush, Megan thought of that someday grandmother—if only she would not misplace one of her grandchildren.

"And Edward."

"Oh, and Mr. Tothwell."

"And Mrs. Bodkins."

"Oh Lord, and Uncle Josepheth."

"And Jamison," Justin murmured wryly, looking pointedly toward the door.

Megan, at first confused, tipped her head back. Justin was right. There stood her old retainer, upside down. His expression was the most proper; his air, however, suggested strong disapproval at the discovery of his mistress and the Earl comfortably prone upon the floor. Furthermore, it could be seen the Earl was holding the Lady much too close.

"And Jamison," Megan sighed.

"Tea, Madame, in five minutes," that worthy announced and closed the door.

"Only five minutes? Madame, that is an eminently wise butler of yours."

"Oh, very wise. I employ only the best servants."

"And so do I, Madame—except for one, that is." His voice took on Uncle Josepheth's tones. "Mad as bedlam, she is. Why, the chit nearly unmanned me once. Sliced at me with a poker, she did."

"Never say so?" Megan declared in mock horror. "Well, I'm glad she didn't. Achieve her aim, that is. Pray, what do you intend to do with this impertinent maid—dismiss her?"

"No. Something much more severe. I intend to

223

shackle her to me for life—and hide every blasted fire
iron, skillet, pot, sword, broom—"

"But you will have nothing left in your house then,
my Lord."

"Indeed, there will be just you and me."

"Yes, my Lord," Megan chuckled.

"Faith, I finally got the maid to agree with me!"
Justin laughed. Soon a symphony of laughter swelled
from the parlor.

Jamison stood discretely outside the door. The tea
cooled in its silver pot. Primly, his eyes marked the
minutes passing on his watch; unlike some servants,
Jamison was excellent, as well as wise.